BRING ON THE BAND

Books by
LLOID AND JUANITA JONES
Published by The Westminster Press

Holiday Mountain
Sentinel in the Saddle
Bring On the Band

BRING ON
THE BAND

by
LLOID AND JUANITA JONES

Philadelphia
THE WESTMINSTER PRESS

Library of Congress Catalog Card Number: 53–5304

PRINTED IN THE UNITED STATES OF AMERICA

To

the thousands of high school students everywhere who cher-
ish their experience as a member of the band, and to their
parents who have provided them with instruments and music
lessons and support and encouragement, this story is
dedicated

WE acknowledge with appreciation the help of Mr. Lowell Kessler, who guided us through abandoned Colorado mines, instructed us in geology and mining engineering, lent us valuable volumes from his professional library, and spent countless hours editing the mining thread of this story for technical accuracy. Without him, the lost Mule Ear vein could never have been opened up again.

CHAPTER 1

J EFF MILES's young sister shouted in his ear, "Do we *have* to sit right here?"

"Why not?" Jeff shouted back. "What would a football game be without a band?"

"Less deafening," Virginia retorted.

A tremendous blare and boom across the aisle to their right marked the climax of "Fight on, fight on for Garrison."

A thousand-throated cheer drowned her words. The Garrison quarterback had just taken a reverse and made first-and-goal-to-go on the opponents' eight-yard line. Down in front the cheerleaders began to bawl through their megaphones: "WE want a TOUCHdown! WE want a TOUCHdown!" The crowd joined in. The cheerleaders yelled: "FEET! FEET!" Everybody, to the last howling partisan crowded onto the topmost plank, began to stamp rhythmically.

Jeff, grinning, got his own number twelves going in the beat set by the wham and thud of bass drum and cymbal. When in Rome, make like the Romans. The same ought to go for Garrison, Colorado.

Stamping here did more than warm the feet too. The wooden stands fairly leaped to life, and the gigantic purple, white-rimmed wall of the Continental Divide in the distance across the valley seemed to go into a jumping jive. You got a sensation that an unstoppable, million-footed horde was rolling *crash-crash-crash* over the opposing team.

Then the jam-packed rooters exploded in a mighty roar. Out on the field striped arms were flung up. On the hand-operated scoreboard somebody replaced a placard. Garrison, 19. Visitors, 0. This school Jeff and Virginia were to enter Monday was one that a student could be proud of.

A whistle shrilled across the aisle, and the band members started to move out from their places, splendid in tailored suits of royal purple with bright markings of gold braid, the Garrison High colors. Cocky caps of purple with an intricate scroll and lyre in gold braid above the bill. Instruments gleamed silver and bronze, or polished wood.

"They're going onto the field for a half-time demonstration," Jeff guessed.

"Look. There are some girls in the band too," Virginia observed. "Isn't that supercilious?"

"Corn's sake!" groaned Jeff. "That word again!" "Supercilious" was the latest special in Ginny's vocabulary. Taken with its sound, she now called everything on the place, from frocks to fried eggs, "supercilious."

"Some girls," he conceded. "I notice the first trumpet is a girl. That real cute brunette there by the tall guy with the sousaphone."

The half-time gun barked. The football players dog-trotted away out of sight under the stands.

The Garrison band lined up back of the north goal posts. Everybody else, Jeff noted, stayed in the stands to watch. High and sweet, trumpet fanfare cut the air. With the last note, the drums set up the marching rhythm. *Dub! Dub-a-dub!* . . . Jeff could scarcely sit still, and indeed he could feel feet tapping the time all through the stands.

8

The band moved out, gleaming in the September sun, stepping a hundred and twenty paces to the minute, instruments at parade rest. Out in front two majorettes, peacock bright, flashed their batons. At a signal from their whistles, instruments were lifted, and the drums ruffled roll-off. The trumpets shouted the exultant opening salute of the "National Emblem" march. The whistles piped again, and the band began to wheel toward the Garrison stands as they played.

Their turning was intricate, an interweaving maneuver Jeff thought was called cross file. And they had scarcely come straight when the majorettes reversed them, so that the whole formation seemed to turn back upon itself. What a show! But the music became somewhat unsteady.

"They kinda messed that up, hunh?" asked Virginia.

"Who do you think they are," Jeff defended, "the Band of America or the U. S. Marines?"

Across the field the band spread out in a bird formation, honoring the Eagle City Warhawks, then regrouped and marched back to face the home stands, taking up positions in the outline of a soldier.

As the crowd rose in tribute to the Garrison Warriors, Jeff and Virginia rose too, though the words of the Purple and Gold song were unknown to them. Not much different, as Jeff heard it, from songs about the Orange and Black, or the Red and White, or the Maize and Blue, to name the colors of a few schools he had attended and could remember offhand. But this song he could learn, once and for all. This one — Jeff crossed his fingers — was for keeps.

Jeff stood watching as the band marched off the field. Man, what an outfit! Sharp. Class like he'd dreamed about since . . . since when? Maybe *too* good, for him. But anyway, for once he was free to try.

9

The players broke ranks and began to make their way back up to their section of the stands. Jeff scanned them closely as they passed.

Suddenly somebody said, "Hello."

It was the girl with the trumpet and the very black hair. She had vivid dark eyes too, and the fairest skin Jeff had seen in this country of ultraviolet rays.

"I'm Carol Hardesty," she went on, "and you're the new kids in our block, aren't you? The Miles. Or Mileses. Which is it?"

Jeff grinned. "Miles and Miles. This is Virginia, and I'm Jeff."

"Hi, Virginia," said Carol Hardesty. "I have a young sister around somewhere too. Oh, there she is! Betty Jean!"

Another chick of practically Ginny's same bounce, as Jeff would have described her, likewise jean-clad, shirt-out, and scarf-covered, detached herself from a knot of girls and joined them. Carol made the introductions.

Betty Jean said: "Sure. You've moved into the old Cloverly place in the middle of our block, and your daddy is going to open up the old Mule Ear Mine, which petered out a long time ago, only maybe he can make it pay again, being a mining engineer. Hunh?"

Jeff took a deep breath. "In a nutshell, yes."

"I'll be in ninth grade," Ginny offered.

"Oh, how swell! So am I. Will you take Latin? All I've learned the first two weeks of school is I'm going to hate Latin. I hope you'll take it."

"Oh, I am," enthused Ginny. "Won't that be supercilious?"

They were joined by a bandsman encircled in the coils of a sousaphone, a tall fellow, slim and blond-haired.

"This is Paul Spencer," said Carol.

"Hiya, Miles." Spencer extended his hand, at the same time giving a quick nod, a chummy wink, and a friendly grin. "Welcome to Garrison, and stuff. Anything I can do to get you started? I'm student body president this year."

Paul Spencer would, Jeff could see, be popular. Looks, and that winning way.

"I really like the band," Jeff said.

"We hope it'll work out," Paul nodded. "A good band means a lot to school spirit, and we hope this year'll be the best ever for Garrison High."

"I've got a puppet show," Ginny was saying to Betty Jean, "as soon as we get it unpacked. I hope you'll come over, since it's practically next door."

The easy manner of Paul Spencer seemed to fade somewhat. "You live close to the Hardestys?" he asked Jeff.

"Six forty-five Spruce."

"Good neighborhood," Paul commented. He placed a hand under Carol's elbow. "Come on, gal. Back to the salt mines. See you around, Miles."

They were gone, leaving Jeff with a feeling of disappointment. He'd had no chance to ask what he wanted to ask about the band. Still, getting connected in a new place took time, as who should know better than he, after so many new places?

Eagle City had no more success during the second half of the game than they'd had the first. Finally it was over, and Jeff and Virginia edged into the press at the ramps.

They reached the family car, and Jeff maneuvered it into Main Street, then up Spruce, "up" meaning exactly that. Garrison, originally a mining center, was an up-and-down town. The streets wound all around to ease the grades, but still a basement on Spruce might be at the level of a first floor on Pine.

Jeff let Virginia out at home, circled the block, and started back toward the football field. The band might not have got away yet, and now that he had at least met two of its members, he was unwilling to wait until Monday to find out what his prospects for band might be.

Carloads of high-schoolers were winding along the streets of the business district, honking to celebrate the football victory. The sidewalks were crowded with students yelling happily. This was the kind of school spirit Jeff liked.

At the stadium luck was with him. A cluster of students carrying instruments came across the parking lot as he arrived, among them Paul Spencer and Carol Hardesty. He drove over and stopped.

"Help with the luggage?" he invited. "Service anywhere in the city."

"Why, how nice," Carol smiled.

"This is Jeff Miles, gang," Paul said. "New guy in town."

"Hi," said Jeff, and received eight assorted hi's and hello's in return. "I think you can all get in," Jeff continued. "The offer of a ride still goes."

"I've got my car," said a burly youth with fiery red hair and innumerable freckles. He nodded his head, and Jeff smothered an exclamation. The car indicated was a two-seated maroon convertible with the top down. Its interior was leather upholstery in the same maroon color, and its exterior gleamed with chrome trimmings. "We're just going up to the Knot Inn for Cokes," the fellow added.

"Let's divide the load and save the springs," Carol suggested. "Come on, Paul. You and I and Mel and Pat can go with Jeff."

They followed her suggestion, and while some climbed in the Miles sedan, the others loaded themselves into the flashy convertible. That vehicle took off with a roar of twin exhausts and a shower of gravel, and was soon out of sight around the corner.

"Boy," said Jeff, "he's out of my class! Like the ant at the picnic, I've got no wings at all, but I'll get there just the same."

The quiet, dark-haired fellow beside Jeff said: "That's Brick Lassiter. Brick always drives as if he'd forgot something and had to go back for it in a hurry. Having his own car, he doesn't have to keep his dad in a mood to let him have it again next Saturday."

The Knot Inn turned out to be a confectionery on Main Street just below Fifth, sandwiched between the Garrison Dry Goods on the corner and the Oro Frozen Food Lockers, which took up most of the middle of the block. The interior of the Knot Inn was paneled with pine, no doubt giving the place its name. It was crowded with high school students, some of them in the swank uniform of the band. Brick Lassiter led the way to the soda bar which extended the length of one side. He turned expansively.

"My treat, gang. Order up."

"Corn's sake!" Jeff was surprised into saying. "You don't mean all of us?"

"Sure!" Big-shouldered Lassiter removed the band uniform cap from his red hair. "Squirrel food! It's on the tab. And it's papa who pays."

Which must mean, Jeff decided, that Brick had a charge account here which his father settled, an unheard-of arrangement so far as Jeff was concerned, and one he couldn't imagine his own dad making. The Lassiters must be enormously wealthy.

Somehow Jeff now felt like an outsider who'd barged in on the gathering to get a free Coke. However, about all he

13

could do was to follow the others, and presently with their sodas and sundaes and root beer floats they all sought seats.

Paul Spencer seated Carol and sat beside her. They were joined by Brick and one of the girls. Crowded as the place was, Jeff and some others remained standing.

Paul's table, Jeff found, soon became the center of the room, notwithstanding its location in a corner. Everybody — but everybody — took occasion to exchange a word with Paul. Everybody knew Paul, and he in turn knew everybody.

It was: " Hi, Chuck, what's the good word? " and: " Hello, Mary Jane, how's geometry? Not going off on any tangents, are you? " and: " How's it, Joyce? Got the assembly all set up for Thursday? "

For everybody, Jeff noted, Paul had the same nod and wink and grin, and he never failed to get an answering smile. Boy, talk about popularity!

During a lull in the reception, Carol asked, " Jeff, what do you go in for, sports? " Basing her guess, perhaps, on his size.

Jeff said quickly, " I'd like to get in the band."

" What's this? " Paul demanded. " You a musician, Miles? "

" No," Jeff disclaimed, " but I've got a horn."

" We're terrifically interested in building up the band this year," Carol told him. " Have you met Mr. Phillips, our director? "

" Not yet," Jeff replied.

" Would you like someone to introduce you? Before your program is arranged Monday? "

" What do you play? " Paul put in.

" Baritone," said Jeff.

" That's too bad." Paul Spencer shook his head thought-

14

fully, seemingly a different person without his nod, wink, and grin. "I'm sorry it couldn't have been alto sax or clarinet. Our baritone section's pretty well set."

"Hear that, Mel?" Brick Lassiter called to the quiet fellow who had ridden over with Jeff. "Miles plays a baritone too!"

"Brick and Mel are the baritones we have now," Paul explained, "about as many as we need for a band our size."

"Mr. Phillips might consider a third one, though, Paul, don't you think?" Carol asked. "The way he's always on the lookout for band talent?"

"Talent!" Brick yelped. "If this guy's talented, he might show us up! Hey, Mel, let's warn him we don't want him if he's good!"

"I'm not good . . ." Jeff began.

"Don't tell Phillips!" Brick cracked. "Let him find out for himself, I always say!"

Following the guffaws brought forth by Brick's remark, Carol said, "It still wouldn't do any harm if I took him to Mr. Phillips and —"

"O.K., O.K.," returned Paul, "but better let me. I'm president of the band. Can you be at school early on Monday, Miles?"

"Boy, can I!" exclaimed Jeff. "But —"

"No trouble." Paul waved airily. Someone else came up to claim his attention, and Jeff couldn't get another word in edgewise.

When Paul rose and said, "Let's break it up, gang; I have to work," the students trooped out to the cars.

Jeff said: "I'd be glad to take you home, those that came with me. Or if there's anybody else . . ."

Mel and Carol and Pat climbed in, and, after a word with Brick, Paul followed. Pat lived well out on Juniper Street. Then Jeff circled back, at their direction, and drove up a hill. The houses here were old, and had something of a run-down appearance except for one. That was set back amidst spacious grounds, well-kept and stately.

"My place," said Mel, nodding toward the big house. "Thanks for the lift, fella. If you make band, I'll see you there Monday."

Did he, Jeff wondered, feel that another baritone coming into the band meant unwanted competition? You couldn't tell by Mel's quiet manner. Had Brick's noisy banter been only kidding? It was an angle to joining a band that had never occurred to Jeff.

"I'll get out at Carol's house," Paul was saying from the rear seat.

"O.K.," said Jeff, "though any place you want to go, I'd be glad to take you before I head home."

"Thanks, but I took her to the game. My job's at the Garrison Theater, easy walking distance from there."

Uh-oh, thought Jeff. He's got an idea I want to barge in on his date. I didn't handle that very smart. Yet he had to grin a little. Fat chance he'd stand, a completely unknown newcomer, against a guy who rated around Garrison the way Paul so clearly did. Not that he'd mind giving it a try if he had any show. He'd never seen a prettier girl than Carol Hardesty.

Jeff pulled up before the corner house in the six hundred block on Spruce, and Paul lifted the ponderous sousaphone from the car. Jeff said, "It was sure swell of you to offer to introduce me to Mr. Phillips."

"That still goes," said Paul. "I'll meet you at school Monday about eight o'clock." But he didn't sound enthusiastic.

"I ought to tell you," continued Jeff, "I haven't had any band experience."

16

"Oh, that so? Well, he may not be able to use you, but we can take credit for not overlooking any bets. See you, Miles. And thanks for the ride." With a hand under Carol's elbow he piloted her up the steps.

Corn's sake! Was he, Jeff wondered, wanted in band or wasn't he? Of all the guys to blow hot and blow cold! If there were reasons, Jeff didn't catch them.

It was good to get home. The Miles home, not the old Cloverly place — Betty Jean Hardesty notwithstanding. 645 Spruce Street was an upright house of dark-red brick, built in the solid, honest style of the years just before the First World War. The Cloverly family had been owners of the custom mill, evidently prosperous but not showy people. When the slump period struck the mining industry, the Cloverlys had closed down the mill and lived on at the house in retirement, lavishing care upon the yard, which was larger than many in Garrison and showed this care. So much Dad had learned from the real-estate dealer.

Jeff climbed the bricked steps from sidewalk to yard level, pausing a moment to feel the homeyness. There had been so many living quarters, so many places, so many hello's and good-by's. But each time he had come up on this wide porch he'd felt a tug inside, as if the sturdy old house said silently, "Here you belong."

Mr. Miles was putting up brackets for the shade to cover the glassed part of the door. He opened to Jeff, his lean, tanned features crinkling in the grin that Jeff had inherited along with his father's height and angular, wide-shouldered build.

"If you could have stayed away a couple of days," Dad kidded him, "we'd have had all the unpacking done."

"I did my best," Jeff retorted. He hung his jacket on the bristly old clothes tree at the foot of the stairs in the entry.

17

"Been down at the Knot Inn with some kids from the high school band."

"Did you like them?" This from Mom, who appeared in the door of the living room.

Jeff grinned at his mother. "Your face is smudged," he teased. Mom was slender, and graceful in her movements, with hair of pure silver which was contradicted by youthful dark eyes. "The point is," he answered her question, "did they like me?"

"Well, did they?"

"The girl that lives up on the corner seems friendly."

"That's Betty Jean Hardesty's sister Carol that I was telling you about," said Ginny, coming in engulfed by a large apron. "I'm getting supper. Why doesn't Jeff ever have to work?"

"Isn't it enough," Jeff asked, "that I have to eat your cooking? Is the next thing to take the wrappings off the chairs?"

"Yes," said Mom. "Who else was at the Knot Inn?"

"The head boy at Garrison High. He's going to take me in Monday to meet the band director."

"You sound pretty well established in town," Dad observed, "for a twenty-four-hour resident."

Thoughtfully Jeff unwound the padding from a chair back. "I guess it's up to me to get going — and Ginny too — after making such a point about always moving around and never getting to be in things while you were working the kind of job you had with Continental Mineral Development."

Dad packed tobacco in his pipe. "Mom and I moved around North America nearly twenty years for Continental Mineral Development. We didn't quit that in order to be noble. We were tired of it too. Besides, you haven't seen the

Mule Ear Mine yet."

"Dinner's ready," announced Ginny. As they sat down she asked, "When *do* we get to see the Mule Ear?"

Their parents exchanged glances. "Why not tomorrow, John," Mom suggested, "while the youngsters are not in school? I couldn't offer much of a picnic, but we could get by."

"Oh, peachy!" exclaimed Ginny. "An expedition!"

"Good idea," Dad nodded. "I could use Jeff's help on the reconnoitering work."

"Let's start early," Jeff requested.

"For once," said Ginny, "O.K. But I warn you I will not be rushed out of this house at the crack of dawn on Monday to get registered at school."

"That's O.K. too," Jeff agreed, "if I can go ahead early by myself. This Paul Spencer is to meet me at eight o'clock, I think."

"Aren't you sure about the time?" asked Dad.

"The fellow didn't seem so eager. They have two baritones already. Then I told him I'd had no experience."

"Pshaw," said Mom. "Wait till they hear you play."

"That's what I'm afraid of." Jeff made a wry face. "I haven't touched the horn since we started to move."

"What are you doing this evening?" Dad inquired dryly.

"O.K.," laughed Jeff. "Right after dinner. Ginny, I'm too starved to be cautious. How about another pork chop?"

"Just don't get supercilious."

"I wish you'd wait to start practicing," said Mom, "until Perry's been fed. The poor dog always howls so when you play."

The big second-floor bedroom that was to be Jeff's in this house surely would be the pleasantest he'd ever had, Jeff thought. After dinner he climbed the stairs to it and sorted through things to find the box of belongings that contained his music and the big black case of his horn. He pried the lid from the box, and then opened the case.

He found he'd put the horn away polished, which was unusually conscientious of him. It was a thing of beauty, not just an upright baritone, but a big-bore, double-belled, five-valve euphonium designed for fullness of tone. The outside was silver-plated, while the mouths of the two bells were finished in gleaming gold. The valves needed a bit of oil, Jeff found, and then their action was fast and clean.

He set up his music stand and got out Otto Langley's *Celebrated Tutor,* ran a scale or two, and did an old favorite exercise that included a lot of grace notes. This was a good room to practice in. No echo.

From the living room below came a lifting, uneasy sound as Perry began to feel the music. Jeff grinned. He thumbed through a book called *Operatic Favorites* until he came to a selection he remembered from *Bohemian Girl,* a heartbreak air titled " Then You'll Remember Me."

As the haunting cadence in the baritone's rich voice filled the room, Jeff lost himself in the music, releasing, somehow, in the cry and the call of the longing melody, all the hopes and doubts he could never put in words.

Up the stairs floated Perry's drawn-out, mournful howl of ancient, elemental, fresh-remembered loneliness.

But in a few minutes Jeff's lip, betraying lack of recent practice, was gone. And then he recalled suddenly tomorrow's trip, and all that it too might mean for the future.

Full of a variety of excitements, he cased his horn and went to bed.

CHAPTER 2

SHADOWS OF DARKNESS and the chill of night still lingered within the deep narrows of Hoodoo Gulch as the Mileses' car labored up the steep windings of the road. But a new sun glinted against the shining green of pine trees and the granite face of cliffs along the heights of the towering slopes above. The cold air was clean, and winy with the tang of balsam. Somehow there was great expectation in the morning.

Jeff, riding in the front seat beside his father, craned to look higher up the mighty hillside. He lost count of the number of mine openings he could see, blacker spots against the shadows, each with its cone-shaped slide of rock and yellowish dirt spilling down the mountain from the tunnel mouth.

"Been a lot of mining along this gulch," he observed.

Dad nodded. "All Hoodoo Mountain is shot through with mineral-bearing veins, like so many sheets of paper placed on edge among a pile of blocks. But the only one that ever had any really high-grade ore was the Mule Ear."

"And it defaulted?" asked Ginny. "Was that what you said?"

Mr. Miles shifted gears, driving with the skill and patience of long experience on mountain roads. "Not quite." He smiled at Ginny through the rearview mirror. "We lost the vein at a fault. A few zillion years ago, as we think, when the world was very young, there came a big crack, lengthwise of this mountain, and half of it slipped downslope."

"That split," Jeff added solemnly, "was a fault, but we don't know whose."

"Oh, corn!" groaned Ginny.

"Anyhow," said Dad, stopping, "here we are. Twenty-two minutes to come five miles. We've made a climb."

They got out quickly and stood gazing in silence across the narrow canyon. Only two things served to distinguish the Mule Ear in appearance from any of the diggings they had passed. It had the largest dump, indicating that it had been worked more deeply, and its portal was a reinforced concrete entrance to the mountain, sign of a big-company operation.

"Let's take our things and go up there," Mom suggested. "I feel as if I want to get as close to that gold as possible."

Ginny added, "After all, here's where Daddy makes our living as long as we're in Garrison."

"Don't sound so temporary," Jeff requested her.

Soon, their arms full, they were all scrambling down to the stream. Mr. Miles was loaded with mining engineer's paraphernalia, Jeff carried the picnic box, while Mom and Ginny brought blankets and extra sweaters and light bits of gear. They crossed the creek on steppingstones and then clambered, breathing heavily, up the sheer, hundred-and-fifty-yard slope of the dump. The sliding, caving mass — big rocks, little rocks, rock dust powdered by drilling and blasting, broken bits of machinery, old tomato cans — made poor walking. Before the tunnel was spread a wide flat built up from the rock and dirt dug out of the mountain.

"I can't wait to go in!" exclaimed Ginny.

"You'll need a light," said Dad, and knelt to pour water into three carbide lamps.

"I'll take the first turn waiting outside," Mom offered, "and keep Perry."

"Can't he go in?" queried Virginia.

"Remember," said Dad, "I haven't been in this mine for nearly fifteen years. Sometimes gases, heavier than air, hang in the bottom of a tunnel. Perry, being close to the ground, might be gassed before our lamps even dimmed as a warning of bad air."

"We could make Perry stay here," Ginny persisted, "if Mom wants to come along."

"One person always stays outside when Dad surveys abandoned workings," Jeff remembered, "to get help in case of a rockfall or something."

"Put on a miner's hat, Ginny," Dad said. "You want metal protecting your head from loose rock that might come down in there."

"I don't know," said Ginny in a small voice, "if I ought to tag along. Maybe I better help Mom."

"Pshaw!" Jeff scoffed. "It'd be dull as dishwater if it was perfectly safe."

"Oh, sure!" returned Virginia. "I was only kidding. Ha, ha."

She picked up one of the small brass lamps, with its feeble-looking candle-sized flame, and the three of them entered the opening in the mountain.

For a dozen of Dad's easy, ambling strides the Mule Ear tunnel was lined, sides and ceiling, with smooth concrete, like a low and narrow basement hall. Then it became simply a rock-lined passageway, along which for a few feet went vague gray light from the portal. Beyond that the light of day was swallowed in a soft, receding cushion of complete

23

blackness. The overarch above them was an endless succession of split-off, irregular surfaces of rock, formless slices from a continuous mass that made a person aware of unnumbered tons of mountain over his head.

The floor was a spongy padding of damp earth, littered with chunks and splinters of rock. Within a short distance they came upon three massive blocks of rock piled across the floor like huge packing cases carelessly dumped. Dad scrambled between and over them.

"Daddy," Virginia inquired, following between him and Jeff, "were you the last one to operate this mine?"

"I managed it for Continental Mineral, if that's what you mean, and nobody has operated it since."

"I must say," complained the girl, "you didn't keep it very clean."

Jeff had, off and on, spent considerable time with his father in various mine workings. Now he explained, "This stuff has fallen in since Dad left." He turned his lamp, which by now seemed amazingly bright, against the wall of the tunnel to show the places from which the chunks of rock had sloughed off. "Remember, there's a lot of pressure on this, all the time."

"There's mud over here," Dad announced. Wearing his mining engineer's coat, its many pockets bulging with equipment, he bulked large and queer-shaped in the flicker of the carbide lamp. "I should have thought to have us put on boots. We'd better go back for them."

Jeff led the return to the portal. As he emerged, Perry came bounding toward him, and Mom looked up, startled.

"Not trouble already," she said.

"We have to have our rubbers," Ginny announced. "It's real gruesome and swell in there, and we have lots farther to go."

Jeff sat down to pull on his rubber boots. The gulch was filled with vast quiet, and drowsy peace, a sense of always. There was something secure, and bountiful, about this friendly earth; part, maybe, of the fascination that holds men to mining.

As they once more filed into the long, narrow darkness, Jeff said, " It still seems odd to me that Continental Mineral abandoned this mine."

" That story I've told you many times," said Mr. Miles.

" Tell it again," requested Ginny. " It seems so much more real, being right here."

" Well, you've heard how I was a young engineer doing survey work for the company and met the old prospector. He was one of the fellows that in those days made their living roaming the hills with a burro, picking up chunks of ore from the surface outcrops of mineral veins. He'd found some rich specimens on this hill, filed this claim, and started to gopher in there where the portal is now."

They scrambled once more over and around the granite spilled across the tunnel.

" You bought the claim for the company," Jeff prompted.

" They bought it on my recommendation," Dad amended. " Then, since it was my find, they put me in charge of its development."

The going was sloppy now, the thin mud sucking at their boots each step they took.

" And it was very good," said Ginny.

" Bonanza vein," agreed Dad. " Averaged a hundred dollars to the ton, and once I sorted out a cement sack of choice pieces that was worth four hundred and fifty dollars, just one sackful. Operating intensively, we took out around a quarter of a million dollars in a pretty short time."

" Where does this go? " demanded the girl, stopping to

peer into a tunnel that led away to the right.

"That's Number One Drift. It just goes back there fifty or sixty feet and stops, where we followed an ore shoot, or branch from the main vein."

"Can I see what's in it?"

"Getting used to being underground, are you?" chuckled her father. "It's all right to investigate if you use caution. There's even another whole set of workings above us that you can look into sometime. But right now I'd like to get on to the end of the main drift."

They moved along, picking their way around heaps of rubble.

Jeff said, "Seems as if the company gave up pretty easily, if the mine had paid so well up till then."

"A company," replied Mr. Miles, "operates on probabilities, just like a big-league team plays percentage ball. When we struck the fault, they sent the chief engineer out to look it over. He figured out the thing to do that offered the best possibility as he saw it. When that didn't pay off, the head office decided to take no more chances."

"I feel a draft," Ginny declared. "How could the wind be blowing in here?"

"Oh, that's Number Five Drift," Dad told her, moving past her into a side tunnel. "There's a raise back there."

They followed the drift for a few feet, and then Ginny exclaimed, "Why, here's a ladder!"

"Seems in good shape too," said Dad, examining it with his light and testing with his hand. The sturdy two-by-six rails and the round oak rungs did not shake.

"It goes down as well as up."

"Yes, we sank a winze here, following another ore shoot. Also a stope — you can see the big space overhead — and as it turned out to be good enough we just drove right on up."

"How far?" asked Ginny.

"About three hundred and fifty feet." Dad grinned. "Clear to the surface. That's where the air is coming from. We got some ore, and it kept the air in circulation, which helped with our ventilation problem. Forty feet up this ladder is the entrance to the second level, that other set of workings I was telling you about."

"How do you remember all those measurements?" Ginny inquired.

"I've memorized all my original maps since we decided to take this venture," Dad answered. "You could check on me by climbing the ladder. The rungs are exactly a foot apart. Forty steps and you're at second level. Three hundred and seventeen more, and you're at the surface."

"What's the point of that?" asked Jeff.

"In a shaft like this your light may blow out, but you can count in the dark."

"And you do mean dark!" remarked Ginny, looking back the way they had come.

They returned to the main tunnel and proceeded farther into the mountain. It became steadily muddier underfoot.

"I wish," said Ginny, "I had seen this Mule Ear vein, so I'd know what it is you're looking for."

Dad turned his light on the tunnel ceiling. "See that queer-looking streak in the rock, that goes all along? That's it."

"That bluish-gray stain? Is that gold? Why didn't you take it out?"

"Couldn't afford to," explained Dad. "It's hardly an inch wide there. Here where we did take it out, it was as wide as my hand. Wider, in places. It costs money for dynamite, and for miners' wages, and for trucks to haul the ore, and for separating the gold from the rock. If you spent fifty dollars for those things and got only five dollars' worth of gold . . ."

" Then," said Jeff, " Continental Mineral didn't make a quarter million dollars' profit? "

" Oh, not by half," said Dad. " The cost of developing it — Well, what do you know about that! "

A slanting heap of rock and dirt confronted them, filling the tunnel from floor to ceiling, ending it completely.

" Is this all? " asked Ginny.

" No, there's about fifty feet more tunnel. There's been a cave-in in the fault zone." Dad held up his light to scan the trace of vein.

" It just stops," Ginny commented, " as if it'd been scissored."

" This is where we lost it," Dad told her. " The part that's in the other half of the mountain is off to one side."

" Which side? " asked the girl.

" To the left. The question is, how far? "

" Why? That's what I could never see," Ginny complained. " I thought you had some way of figuring all that out on your slide rule by climbing over the mountain above a mine."

Dad laughed. " Hoodoo Mountain was so unthoughtful as to hide the surface outcrops of the fault plane and the vein on its far side under rock slopes or trees or something. At least we never found where they outcropped. We had to bore on through the fault zone and then explore to the left."

" You found the vein, though," Jeff prompted.

" We found a vein," amended Dad, " but one that was quite poor and thin. It appeared that the Mule Ear had petered out."

" It wasn't the Mule Ear? "

" I've since become convinced that it wasn't. Some years later another outfit discovered a vein they called the Tally

Ho running parallel to the Mule Ear about three hundred feet off to our right. Their prospecting showed that the Tally Ho was quite poor and thin, and yet mineralogically quite like the Mule Ear. I think now we must have hit the extension of the Tally Ho instead of the extension of the Mule Ear."

"So," said Jeff, "because of the slippage due to faulting, the Mule Ear is three hundred feet farther to the left on the other side of the fault, but still there."

"Two hundred ninety-three feet, as nearly as I can tell."

"And we're just going to dig on that much farther and find it!" exclaimed Virginia.

"That's exactly what we're going to do," Jeff cracked, "but not till after lunch." He returned to the matter at hand. "What about this cave-in?"

"We'll have to clean it out," said Dad. "Here's where we begin our surveying."

He took out his Brunton compass, which Ginny was wont to call "Daddy's compact" because of its size and shape and the mirrors it contained, ingeniously arranged for surveying. Jeff carried one end of a steel tape from place to place as his father directed. Mr. Miles made entries in a black notebook and plotted the survey on a map he produced.

Slowly they worked their way back toward the portal. Jeff's part included many periods of patient waiting. To keep warm in the seeping chill of the mine he accompanied Virginia on numerous little excursions into crosscuts and murky recesses. Regardless of the day or season outside, the temperature in here would remain constantly between forty-five and fifty degrees.

He enjoyed the brief trips, with Ginny peering into the blackness, squealing at made-up dangers. Her imagination, always active at home on her puppet plays, here became

29

loosed completely. Jeff was chuckling at her flights of fancy when Dad called him back.

As they emerged into the sunny noon, they sniffed in appreciation. From the campfire Mom had built came the good fragrance of sizzling bacon and simmering pork and beans.

Her first hunger relieved, Ginny quipped, " Our future looks pretty black, huh? "

Dad laughed. " Pretty busy," he said. " Track to lay, tunnel to clean. Timbering, probably, all the way through the fault zone, which is fourteen feet. Drainage ditch along the hanging wall. I can certainly find plenty for a crew to do."

" One thing," said Jeff, " a crew should be easy to get now. With all these other mines closed down, there must be lots of miners out of work."

" Sounds right," Dad answered, " but it isn't. Gold mining was stopped early in World War II, you know, because gold wasn't needed in arms plants. Finding any experienced man will be a piece of luck."

" I guess black future wasn't funny," said Ginny. " Excuse me."

Mr. Miles said: " Oh, it's an ill wind. If mining had been active in the region, somebody else would have got the Mule Ear. I wouldn't have found it kicking around ownerless and been able to get it for taxes."

" If that's good," Jeff ventured.

" It is," declared Dad. " I've always wanted to work the Mule Ear again, my way. The more experience I got, the more I've been convinced I was right. All the professional papers since have predicted further values at greater depth here. If I could have had two more months . . ."

Ginny said, " You mean we'll strike gold in two months? "

"Not now, Ginny. Conditions have changed. Be more like six months, maybe, or even, allowing for some bad luck, a year."

"A year!" Mom exclaimed, and then stopped.

Jeff understood. Until the Mule Ear began to pay, there would be no income for the Miles family. Only the savings accumulated during the long years of their wanderings. The family's living had to come from savings, and so did the capital to develop the mine. Would the savings stand this double drain for a whole year?

"Meantime," Dad said briskly, "we have a permanent home, and a chance to do all the settling-down things we've always wanted to do. Best setup we've ever had."

Jeff had nearly forgotten that. Up here the family and their twenty mountainous acres seemed like a whole world. A new school to enter, a band to try out for, friends to make among kids like Paul Spencer and Brick Lassiter and the Hardesty girls — those things were remote, almost unreal.

Jeff returned to the tunnel with his father while Mom and Ginny cleared away after the meal. Perry followed them for a time, but later disappeared. Probably, they decided, the dog had grown tired of the darkness and gone back out.

"Oh, how snorky!" Ginny's voice exclaimed suddenly. "You can write on the rocks."

They turned to see her moving her lamp, the flame held close to the tunnel wall.

"We often mark locations with a carbide lamp," Dad informed her.

"You see Perry?" Jeff asked.

"Yes. He came out and is hanging around with Mom. Look. Street sign."

She had spelled out, in sprawled, smudged, black letters: "DEAD-END DRIVE."

Dad laughed. "O.K. for now. But when we get that cave-in mucked out, you'll have to change the name."

"Oh, could I put names on all the things, Dad?" she bubbled. "Like 'Murder Alley' and 'Dreadful Drift' and so on? Would it bother your working, I mean?"

"I doubt," chuckled her father, "if I'd confuse your markings with mine. Go ahead."

"I know just the place to call 'Bash-in Boulevard,'" Ginny enthused, and her voice trailed away as she hurried off. Presently the wavering glow of her carbide lamp disappeared around a turn.

As their work took them the way she had gone, they came upon another sign: "South Midnight Court." Farther on they reached a litter of fallen rubble.

"Look," laughed Dad. "'Brain Squsher Junction.' Original spelling too."

"Also cheerful," Jeff grinned.

They went once more to the cave-in, so Dad could verify the size of the first timber set. It seemed to Jeff that the amount of work grew more appallingly huge with each entry into Dad's notebook.

Finally he asked, "Isn't there a risk that you might do all this and still not find a paying ore deposit?"

"Yes," Dad said readily. "There's plenty of chance in any mining. Also in any other business, don't forget. Men have gone broke in grocery stores and banks too."

Jeff straightened the tape and drew the slack out of it. "That's usually when they didn't know enough about the business, isn't it?"

"Sometimes, I suppose. At least I wouldn't know enough about those lines to be successful in one of them. Mining I do know."

"So it's not really a chance."

32

"I didn't say that," Dad returned. "Less chance than if I didn't know what I was doing, let's say. But of course there's the possibility, always, that the Mule Ear may turn out to be a bust, a *borrasca,* as the old Spanish miners used to say."

Jeff inquired cautiously, "Then what?"

"Oh, say, now! Your imagination is getting as bad as Ginny's. I think we'll call this enough for today. Want to carry some of these tools?"

It was a relief to emerge onto the sunny flat after all those hours in that crowding darkness. They found the picnic box neatly packed and Perry barking at a chipmunk from the foot of a nearby tree.

While Dad emptied the carbide lamps, Jeff got the box. Together they went down the slope, Perry plunging ahead. They saw Mom open the car door and the dog disappear inside, intent as always on claiming his place by the back window.

Back to town now, Jeff thought. Tomorrow he and Ginny would be doing *their* exploring of new possibilities. He wished there could be some kind of compass or table of logarithms they could use.

"Where's Ginny?" Mom inquired as Jeff and Mr. Miles arrived.

"Ginny! We thought she was here with you."

"I didn't see her come out," Mom answered. "I supposed she was with you." Mom got out of the car, and the three of them turned rapidly toward the mine.

"She was giving names to all the hidey holes," said Dad. "We probably passed her without her knowing." He explained about "Murder Alley" and "South Midnight Court."

"With that kind of project on, she'd lose all sense of time." Mom's voice was equally matter-of-fact.

33

Jeff lunged upward along the sliding slope. He'd been in on emergencies before and knew those especially calm tones of his parents. At the portal he bellowed, " Ginny! " But his breath was gone, and between the echoes and the hammering of his heart he could not have heard an answer.

" I'll get the lamps going," Dad said behind him. " No use calling until we're farther in."

They went beyond the trace of natural light before Dad drew a deep breath and sent his full bass rolling. " Virginia! O Ginny! " The words echoed cavernously, faded to silence.

They passed " Spook Speedway," and eventually " Dead-End Drive," but their shouts brought no answer except their own echoes.

" Dad," said Jeff, " that raise."

" We'll check," Dad agreed. " Number Five Drift is just ahead."

Where the tunnels divided, they spelled out, in large, crooked letters, " POINT OF NO RETURN."

" Oh, no! " gasped Mom. " After that, it would be pure melodrama if she wasn't all right."

" I wish we'd brought Perry," Jeff muttered. " He might follow her scent."

" She's been everywhere," Dad said. " He'd only go at random. Ginny! "

" The ladder's just ahead," said Jeff. " Corn's sake! "

It was like a black, crooked grin upon the wall: " DEATH DROP." And a wavering arrow indicated the yawning gap of the winze.

" We were talking about the ladder," Jeff remembered. By this time cold was crawling up his spine. Those crazy names! If the kid had had some weird premonition . . .

" Ginny! " Dad had cupped his hands and was shouting

down the winze. He turned upward and yelled, "Virginia, where are you?"

Hollowly, "*Are you . . . are you . . . are you,*" came back at them. Mom's light blew out in the air current, and Jeff relighted it from his lamp.

"Listen!" he hissed.

It was faint, but it wasn't an echo! "Here! Here I am, Daddy . . . *addy . . . addy . . . addy!*" Small and high and incredibly far away.

"Stay still!" Dad shouted. "Which way did you go?"

"Upstairs. Forty ladder rungs upstairs. Only my light went out. I don't know which way is the ladder."

"Don't move!" Dad called again. "Stay there! I'm coming!" He swung onto the ladder, adjusted the lamp on his cap, and climbed rapidly out of sight into the far reaches above.

It must have been only a minute, though it seemed like ages, before he reappeared, guiding Virginia's feet on the steps.

"I had 'Hairpin Boulevard' marked," she said, uncertainly, "and I was going to call the shaft 'China Way,' and then my light went out, and it was so doggone dark — "

Suddenly she broke into sobs and rushed for Mom. Mrs. Miles comforted her for a moment and then brought a cleansing tissue from her pocket. Ginny blew her nose loudly.

"Jeff," the girl demanded, "what are you doing?"

"Just helping out with names," he answered, and stepped back.

Ginny quavered unsteadily, "You're a supercilious jerk!"

He had lettered blackly on the wall: "LOST CHE – ILD LANE."

35

CHAPTER **3**

ARLY MONDAY MORNING Jeff departed for school, leaving
Virginia to come on later. He was just as glad, for he was in
no mood for sprightly chatter. This was too important, and
too unknown. How, he wondered now, could he have been
so fascinated by bands for so many years and still have learned
practically nothing of their inner workings, like tryouts, and
rehearsals, and all that? Uncertainty weighed down his
middle almost as heavily as the thirty pounds of cased euphonium weighted his arm.

The front door of the school was locked and Paul Spencer
was nowhere in sight. Maybe he wouldn't show up. That
might be for the best. Jeff felt far from ready for any musical
test. He'd tried to practice again last night, but after the
long day and the strenuous excitement, he still felt dragged
out this morning.

"Hiya, Miles." That was Spencer, with his flashing nod,
wink, and grin. "Just occurred to me you might be here.
Can't get in this door yet. Come around by the gym."

Jeff picked up his horn. Paul led the way to a recessed
entrance and into the venerable gray stone building. Inside,
they climbed stairs to a running track which circled above a
gym. At the far side of the gym a wide gallery opened off the
running track. Across the gallery was a door on which was

lettered the word " BAND." By this time Jeff was thinking that if he had a carbide lamp he could imagine himself in the labyrinth of the Mule Ear Mine. Paul knocked on the door.

From the room a voice called, " Come in."

It was a great square room, walls and ceiling patterned with rectangles of sound-absorbing fiberboard. There was a confusion of chairs and music stands, and along a rear wall wooden racks for instrument cases. From a desk near the door Mr. Phillips, the band director, rose.

" Good morning."

Jeff had his first near look at the director. The man gave a different impression from that of Saturday, when Jeff had seen him in uniform at the front of the band. Medium height. Very lean. Intense blue eyes. Sandy hair that thinned on top. Small clipped mustache.

Paul favored the director with his nod, wink, and grin. " How's it, maestro? Hope we're not interrupting."

" Meaning you know you are," drawled Mr. Phillips, " and hope you can get away with it." Mischief tugged at the strong features and twinkled in those sharp eyes. " Well, you can."

" I've made a discovery," Paul breezed on unabashed. " This is Jeff Miles. He's just entering school. Junior."

Mr. Phillips shook Jeff's hand cordially. " Any friend of our distinguished first citizen," he declared, face solemn, " is — ah — well, anyway. What's the discovery, Paul? "

" Jeff plays baritone," Paul announced.

" No! I supposed he carried that black box because he eats an unusually big lunch."

Jeff couldn't help laughing, and the tension inside him eased. He was vaguely astonished at this teacher-student conversation, but too concerned with his own fate to think about it much.

"I know we've got baritones this year," Paul went on. "But next year, Mel will be graduated, and with Brick the only horn in that section, I thought maybe — "

"I thought maybe the baritones could stand additional strength," Mr. Phillips interrupted, "this year. On occasion. Let's see your horn, Jeff."

As Jeff stooped to open the case, Paul asked, "Is it a double-barreled one like that three-hundred-and-fifty-dollar job of Brick's?"

Jeff was startled into speech. "Oh, no, it wasn't that expensive! It has the double barrel, and it's a good horn, I think, but I got it reconditioned. My tenth birthday present."

"It *is* a good horn," Mr. Phillips commented, looking at the manufacturer's name engraved on the big bell. "If," he added dryly, "it's played that way. You've been studying for seven years?"

"Well, off and on," Jeff said uncomfortably.

Mr. Phillips asked, "What band experience have you had?"

"I've never played in a band."

Mr. Phillips sat down. "Let's hear a few long tones."

Jeff placed the mouthpiece to his lips and played a scale, sustaining each note for sixteen counts. When he lowered his horn, Mr. Phillips was leaning forward, looking at him oddly.

"Could you do a scale in eighths at a speed of, say, ninety?"

Jeff raced up and down three times in sharp staccato, then paused for breath.

"Hit the open tones from bottom to top," ordered Mr. Phillips. "I said 'hit,' but take your time."

His right hand withdrawn from the valves, Jeff tongued forth the notes. He had grave doubts about the high ones. He

38

was out of practice. Each tone he gave his best.

The high B-flat came out with a blast that sent a rattle through the strings of a snare drum in the instrument racks. Jeff felt red mount in his face.

"Paul, loosen that snare, will you?" Mr. Phillips rose to rummage in a wall cabinet of shelves thick-stacked with music. He turned to Jeff with a small brown book, which he opened and placed on a stand. "Let's see if you can read." The book was opened to "El Capitan."

Jeff hesitated, but decided not to say anything. After all, he could use any lucky break. He swung into the strains of "El Capitan" with every bit of skill he possessed. He had done the trio once and was crashing the breakup when Mr. Phillips raised a hand.

"Would you mind telling me," the director inquired, "what goes on here? You're not sight reading."

Jeff explained: "'El Capitan' is one of my favorites. I know it by heart."

"I thought you'd never played in a band."

Well, this was it. If only Paul, who was eying him queerly, could develop sudden urgent business elsewhere! Jeff fumbled out words.

"It sounds goony. I've always been crazy about a band — concert, parade, games, anyplace. Radio. Records. Finally I got myself a book like this, so I could play along with the records. Screwball, I know, but it was only for kicks."

"The instructors you've had worked with you along this line?" asked Mr. Phillips.

Jeff shook his head. "I never told 'em. Mostly they used the Langley book, because I had it. Some teachers advised me to join the school band, but we've moved around a good deal. I never could count on being in a place long enough, till we came here."

"Does that mean you've learned precision tempo and dynamics just listening to the radio?"

"And recordings," Jeff said. "You can play records over till you get the hang of a thing. Then for kicks I'd see if I could stay with a live band on the radio when that number happened to be on the program."

"Now," drawled Mr. Phillips, "I've heard everything." He leaned far back in his swivel chair. Presently he said to Paul: "Look, you go be the people's choice someplace. You've done your school a notable service this morning, and can quote me on that."

Paul withdrew, seeming to move reluctantly. The look on his face was unreadable, to Jeff. At the door he flashed his nod, wink, and grin and said jauntily, "Thanks, maestro," and was gone.

"This band," Mr. Phillips said thoughtfully, "could use another baritone — in the director's opinion, if not the head boy's. I think you play well enough. The question is whether you can fit into the organization. You can't switch us off with a twist of the wrist."

"I know, sir," Jeff said. "What I'm most afraid of is that I won't be able to follow your baton."

"Don't ' sir ' me," grinned the director. " That'd mark you as a stranger in this country. You'll catch on to following the stick. What I mean is getting along with the youngsters. The one thing a band has to be is together. Had any experience in teamwork — like sports, for instance?"

"No," said Jeff, refraining from "sir." "We've moved around too much for me to make the team anywhere. Boxing. Skiing. But no team sports."

"Um-m. Well, just don't be the unfriendly type, and do the best job you can with your horn. You'll get to be one of us as you show you can carry your share of the load."

While Jeff put his horn in the case racks, Mr. Phillips penned something on a slip of paper. He handed Jeff the slip and opened the door. " This is for the office," he said.

Jeff stopped short.

Clustered there in the gallery was a knot of students. There must have been twenty, and they all looked at him. It made him feel like a criminal in a police line-up. As he gathered himself and moved on, he saw that they all carried instruments which they'd been waiting to put in the band room, and the flash of self-consciousness seemed a little silly. Two or three kids nodded to him, vaguely. Maybe at the Knot Inn —

" Sounded good to me," said someone, and he saw it was Carol Hardesty, smiling. " Are you in? "

" I guess I am." He looked at the slip from Mr. Phillips: " *Jeff Miles — take band 7th hour — H. M. P.*"

He heard Carol say, " Congratulations," as she walked on into the room.

Suddenly the full meaning of it came to him. He was in! *Jeff Miles take band!* Years of hope and longing, of visioning himself stepping smartly in a dashing uniform, and now he was in! It was happening! He wanted to leap high, whirl himself around in mid-air, and yell, " *Ya-hoo* " at the top of his lungs.

He came partly back to earth, enough to test the maze of corridors and eventually find the office on the second floor. There was Ginny, and she had brought Mom, and both were being piloted, apparently, by Betty Jean Hardesty.

He slapped the paper on the counter in front of Mom. " Get a load! " he exulted in tones suppressed by respect for the office.

The girls peered too, going into excited squeals similarly subdued, and Mom said, " Well, Jeff, fine! " She patted his shoulder warmly. " I know Dad'll be pleased too." Though she sounded as if she'd expected as much all along.

After some goings-on which Jeff heard only through a suffused warm glow, he emerged from the office carrying a *Student's Handbook* and a program card enrolling him in band and some other subjects. Almost immediately he saw Paul Spencer, across the hall, standing in a widening where there were bay windows. Jeff started across.

Betty Jean's voice stopped him. " That's Senior Circle. The *Handbook* says freshmen, sophomores, and juniors are not encouraged to go there. The low-down is, keep out."

So Jeff did not carry out his intention to say, " Thanks! " to the head boy. He tried to catch Paul's eye, to wave appreciation, but Spencer was deep in talk with two other guys, Brick Lassiter and Mel Price. The two baritones. Was that only chance? Somehow Jeff's suffused glow lost a degree of its warmth.

He went to various rooms and enrolled in classes. There were teachers who presented lessons, and students who recited, no doubt. Jeff wouldn't have known.

Dad was at home for lunch, and it was a happy noon hour for the family. Ginny was excited at being in high school, her first experience with elective subjects. And everybody shared the elation over Jeff's prospects in band.

" Even I had a break this morning," grinned Dad. " Found a gold miner. Young fellow, Mexican, named Tony Vasquez."

" I thought Mexicans did farming and kept sheep," said Virginia. " Things like that."

" Tony is working for a farmer right now," Dad told them. " But he comes of a long line of miners. Remember, the first gold taken out of these mountains was mined by Mexicans, and those that still follow it are some of the best

42

miners we have. Anyway, this lad is looking for an opportunity to get ahead, and I think we're going to be able to work out something."

Everything, Jeff thought as he returned to school, seemed to be turning out hopefully for the family in Garrison. Almost too good to be true. It seemed like no time, in a way, and in a way like forever, until his sixth-hour class was finished and he was once more searching out the gym running track, making his way around in front of the bleachers and entering the band room.

His first glimpse of band practice hit him with a jolt of surprise. Kids were swarming all over the room, arranging chairs and warming up instruments with a deafening cacophony of tootles and tweets and oomps and pahs topped off by the ruffle and thud of drums. Everything was uproar and confusion, and nobody paid any attention to him.

Not knowing what he should do, Jeff stood against the wall out of the way, his program card in hand. How many times before in his life had he stood so, aside, awkward and unfamiliar, while everybody else acted — was — right at home! Only, maybe, this was the last time, if he could, as Mr. Phillips said, learn to get along, show them he'd carry his share of the load. He'd do more than his share gladly, if he could be one of them.

Mr. Phillips, striding by, stopped long enough to take the card and call above the din, " Get your horn."

Jeff went to the instrument racks, glad of something to do. As he inserted the mouthpiece and adjusted the bells to playing position, he heard, faintly, the sound of a bell ringing. Immediately came a terrific shrill whistle blast, and the noise stopped abruptly and completely. You could almost feel echoes in the silence.

" I have Carter, Miller, Stone, and Wiley marked absent,"

a throaty voice called. Jeff saw, then, a girl standing on the little director's platform at the front of the room. Rather a small girl and strikingly pretty despite too much make-up.

" I'm here," some fellow said.

" Miller present but misplaced," the girl said tartly, and made an erasure in a book she held. Jeff noticed she wore a whistle on a cord about her neck, and realized that she was one of the majorettes he had seen with the band Saturday. Must double as secretary.

Now she held up his program. " The new fellow is Jeff Miles, and he plays baritone. A junior, it says here."

" Yay, juniors!" someone called, and there was an immediate response of yay's and boo's mixed with laughter.

" You'll sit here, Jeff," said Mr. Phillips, " next to this drab character we call Brick Lassiter."

" Stop-Light Lassiter," someone threw out.

Lassiter half rose with a defiant, " Ah, shaddop!" That drew a laugh, during which Jeff managed to slip into the chair at Brick's right. He wondered if the " stop-light " crack referred to Brick's fiery hair or his driving of the maroon convertible. At Brick's left sat Mel Price.

Mel smiled at Jeff and said in an undertone, " Hi, feller." Brick muttered, " Howya?" Jeff nodded, relieved they didn't sound resentful of him. Brick's horn was a resplendent instrument, gleaming gold with pearl-tipped valves and ornate scrollwork engraving.

A tall, awkward girl in steel-bowed spectacles, whom Mr. Phillips called Henrietta, brought Jeff a thick folder of music. Then she slid into a chair in front of the stand and picked up a French horn. The two majorettes withdrew, carrying their batons, probably to practice twirling in the hall.

At this point Paul mounted the stand, magnificently encircled by the intricacies of the sousaphone, its gleaming bell standing out showily above his sunny hair. Jeff thought, oddly, of the horned monarch of an elk herd.

"We always start with a concert C-scale in whole notes to tune up, Miles," Paul said.

Jeff nodded, though Paul's words somehow revived the old feeling of being a stranger in a strange land.

At a motion of Paul's left hand, all instruments came up from laps to playing positions. They started the scale in unison, solid and sustained. At G, Paul made a cutting motion. They stopped.

"The A, Bill," Mr. Phillips said from the rear, and the oboe player sounded forth. The director moved among the trombones, adjusting tuning slides.

After a few more notes they stopped again while Mr. Phillips supervised relocation of mouthpieces in the reed section. Jeff began to see the function of Paul as a stand-in for the director while he worked among the players.

Tuning completed to his satisfaction, Mr. Phillips went to the stand and Paul to his place among the basses. Everything had become business now. No more tootling. No wisecracking. Mr. Phillips called the name of a march.

It was that old favorite, "Washington Post." Jeff hardly needed the music to play his part. But with the crash of the opening salute he found himself confused. This did not sound like a band sounded from an amplifier. There was a solid wall of trombone behind him. Off to his right he could hear the bass. Somewhere, trumpets seemed to be going down another street, and across the way some clarinets played toward him. When he waited for the exclamatory thud of the drum, it came from far away. The baritone part he couldn't hear at all.

He puffed along, careful not to call attention to himself by playing full out. He began to understand what was happening. From outside, a band gave a whole effect. Seated in it, you heard an agglomeration of separate airs fitted one on another.

As in the trio. He could hear the trumpets snapping out cleanly their catchy little triple-time melody. The baritones were supposed to lift and soar above, coming down to join the trumpets as they entered the breakup strain. Only the soaring didn't come off, or at least Jeff didn't hear it. The lack bothered him like a missing tooth.

When they leaped out of the breakup to repeat that strain, Jeff could hold back no longer. On the boom of the drum he took a low breath, filled his big horn, and raised the counter-melody high and clear above the trumpets' heads as he had in practice with the record player. So the piece really sounded to him like "Washington Post."

Mr. Phillips glanced sharply in his direction, and Carol, sitting immediately at the director's right, half turned in her chair. Jeff suddenly felt conspicuous, but in a second they were again at the crashing breakup strain, where the sheer volume of sound swallowed up individuals.

At the end of the march Mr. Phillips leafed through the music on his stand, then looked up and called, "'Orpheus.' Take 'Orpheus in the Underworld.'"

This was a different matter. Jeff had heard the Offenbach overture, but he had never seen the music before. And the manner of rehearsal changed quickly. After a dozen bars Mr. Phillips whacked the stand with his stick. All playing stopped.

"Look," he said, "we're telling a story. There's this nice guy Orpheus. Has a girl friend. Beauteous babe. Along comes this slimy character from the underworld and sn-n-natches her. Menace. Get it? Menace me, basses! Second valve."

46

Upon this vivid description the basses rolled menacingly. Mr. Phillips cried, "Ah! Ah!" in evident satisfaction. In all his experience, Jeff had never come upon a teacher like Mr. Phillips. But then, he reflected, he had never taken band anywhere else, either.

They worked it out, phrase by phrase. Amazing, to Jeff, how Mr. Phillips, with countless meaningful gestures of his left hand and varied posturings of his lean body, made the music come alive, fairly lifted all sections into their parts.

Then Jeff saw a double line, over which was printed: "Lento. Baritone solo." He lowered his horn, waiting to see whether Mel or Brick played the passage. But both continued, and the trombones behind took the same notes. In a moment Mr. Phillips whacked the stand again.

"Nope," he said. "Nope. Nope. Too heavy. Lay out, trombones. I know you're cued in, but it drowns me. All the baritones take it together. Brokenhearted, now. That's what Orpheus is. Mourn!"

Jeff had caught the way of it. Longing, reaching, calling, like the number from *Bohemian Girl*. Not difficult, except for one high note occurring at intervals. He gave the yearning cadence all his best.

"Elegant!" cried Mr. Phillips in that stirring tone. "Elegant!" Jeff glanced up at him.

Their next note was the high A-flat. Jeff tried for it hastily. For a split second no sound came. Then came a quavery, sputtery wheeze that was first too high, then too low, and then nowhere at all. Out of practice! Cheese!

Every eye in the place abruptly was turned on Jeff, all playing stopped, and he would have welcomed a collapse of the floor beneath him. His face was burning and no doubt as red as Brick's hair. Corn's sake! Why had he ever thought he could play in a band?

47

The director's lean features showed that dry grin. "Get your mouth made up the same as your mind there, Bub," Mr. Phillips advised, and everybody burst into laughter. "Now all you jokers that never missed a note yourselves keep on laughing, and the rest go back to the lento."

They did, all but Brick. From the corner of an eye, Jeff saw the redhead give three silent, exaggerated haw-haw-haw's before he started to play. Which bothered Jeff.

"Play right out, baritones!" Mr. Phillips called sharply.

Jeff caught the next note, played desperately to redeem himself. The first day, and he'd really fixed himself up! Why had he ever —

They finally reached the end of the overture, and Mr. Phillips announced: "Marching practice. Game Saturday with Lamont."

Everybody got up and started trooping toward the door. The girl Henrietta approached Jeff. "We take only the little brown book. Do you have a lyre? Or we have some clothespins."

"I have a lyre," Jeff mumbled. "Thanks."

He went to his case for the lyre. By the time he got it, the last players were crowding out the door. Jeff followed, down a short stairway and through another door onto the recreation field. The band members were forming lines, and the majorettes were at the front, acting very much in charge. Having no assigned place here, Jeff stopped and waited.

"Hey, Mr. Phillips," called the secretary-majorette, "where shall we put the big guy?" Making, it seemed to Jeff, a general point of it.

"Baritones in second rank," Mr. Phillips replied. "Let's see. How many in the band now, Rosie, counting Jeff?"

"Sixty-three," Rosie told him promptly.

"And what times what equals sixty-three?" Without

waiting for a reply, Mr. Phillips moved to the rear of the band, changing this player and that, arranging them by sevens. Some mutterings arose, and Jeff became definitely uncomfortable. He could understand their not liking to shift all around solely on his account.

" All right, Jeff," said Mr. Phillips. " Second rank, middle file. Here."

Jeff moved to the center of the second row. Brick was on the right end of the line, directly behind Paul, who occupied the most important position at the right front. The two were talking together in undertones.

Mr. Phillips said sharply, " Break it up, fellows! "

" Mr. Phillips," Rosie called again in her carrying, parade-ground voice, " Jeff's too tall to be in the middle."

Distinctly, but in an undertone, Brick could be heard to say: " Sure. Let's be sure to take care of Jeff! "

Mr. Phillips directed his dry grin at Brick. " You're right, Rosie. Jeff should be right guide, Mel in the middle, and Brick on left end. Make that change, fellows."

Corn's sake! Jeff groaned inwardly. *Not Brick's position!* Brick's face was dark and his eyes furious as they passed. Jeff didn't get a good look at Mel.

The drums started to beat time. Jeff glued his eyes to Paul's back. He'd do everything Paul did, and maybe get by without more special attention.

They moved fifteen or twenty yards, and the whistle shrilled. One, two, three, four — it blew again. Paul pivoted on his heel and stepped to his left. Jeff, following his every move, wasn't a watch tick late in doing the same.

" Oops! "

Somebody plowed full into Jeff. He lost his balance, stumbled against Paul. Both whistles piped frantically. Everybody stopped, amidst noise and confusion.

Through the noise, though, and his own rattled senses, Jeff heard Paul grate out, as if exasperated beyond enduring, " Do you always have to be an eager beaver, Miles? "

" As you were! As you were! " Rosie was shouting.

And suddenly she was beside Jeff, a hand on his elbow. " Never marched before, hunh? " Her throaty voice lifted above the rip and boom of the drums. " I'll show you. Don't do anything till you get to where Paul was when he did it."

The other majorette guided the band, and Rosie piloted Jeff, good-naturedly explaining things, maneuvering him out of harm's way. He'd been prepared to hate this female top sergeant and her raucous voice. Now he looked on her with sincere gratitude — and hopeless envy of her springy, rhythmic step invariably in faultless time.

Somewhere a bell jangled, or maybe it was only a ringing in Jeff's ears. No, school was out, thank fortune! Whereupon Jeff learned more about the band. The end of school made no difference. The slamming drums never missed a beat.

Jeff saw from the corner of his eye kids drifting out of the building, loitering on the sidewalk to watch the band practice. He remembered days when he had stood so, wistful. Now, ironically, he almost wished he were back among the onlookers.

They did at least a thousand turns and reverses and wheel-arounds, until Jeff was totally numb. They played " Military Escort " and " National Emblem " until he was sure the mouthpiece bouncing around his face had left him fewer than twenty teeth. Rosie's shoes and socks became gray with dust, but her movements lost not a bit of their magnificent co-ordination.

They practiced the routine of getting into and out of the soldier formation for the Garrison Warriors. They formed the letters *L–A–M–O–N–T*. You couldn't, Rosie declared, do a tiger formation for the Lamont Tigers that looked like anything but the Big Dipper with cymbals on its tail. Jeff learned to find his place in the letter *A*, thinking that was well along in the alphabet for anybody so dumb as he. He learned the baritone part in "Come On, You Tigers." And, most important, he didn't run afoul of Paul or Brick again.

At a quarter of five they came to a halt. Mr. Phillips asked: "Can you make it early in the morning, Jeff? We'll see about a uniform for you."

Jeff said, "Yes, sir."

He slogged home, dragging lead in his shoes. Homework. Practice. Early tomorrow. Corn's sake! When did a guy live? Or was that only if you didn't take band?

He set down his horn case beside the old hat tree, dog-tired and half starved. Ginny promptly descended the stairs, with sound effects like an empty barrel rolling down the steps.

"How'd you like band?" she demanded.

Jeff was nearly beyond speech. He remembered dimly that once he had been on top of the world because he'd made band. It excited the family, it was an achievement for him, it held great promise for the future. Right now he couldn't recall why.

"Like band?" he repeated heavily. "Just dandy! It reminds me so much of Valley Forge!"

CHAPTER 4

Regularly on Saturday mornings Jeff helped at the
Mule Ear Mine. He was glad he had the chance, as he reflected one morning after he had been in the band about a
month. Mine work was simple and uncomplicated — at
least the kind he did — a welcome change from the tense-
ness that had come to hover over school and band. Wielding
pick and shovel, a person could always see what he was
accomplishing and know where he stood.

Right now he stood in four inches of oozing mud mixed
with rock from the size of gravel to chunks as large as his
head, scooping the stuff into an ore car. He had two lamps
to relieve the impenetrable blackness, one mounted on the
front of his metal hat, the other, a Wolf lamp, hooked on a
projection of rock. By this light he saw that the car, an
iron box on four flanged wheels to ride the rails of the
narrow track, was now practically full. That meant he had
shoveled nearly a ton of muck since eight o'clock, but he
had advanced the drainage ditch alongside the track by
almost ten feet. That was a satisfaction.

Out of the solid dark came another wavering light. A
hearty voice called, " How you doing, Cousin Jack? "

" Ready to roll," Jeff answered, smiling at the name.
Cousin Jack was the title always given to any of the Cornish

miners who had come to this country out of England seventy-five years ago, and who were everywhere known as masters of their trade.

"I've got a load too," said Tony Vasquez, becoming visible now behind the ore car he was pushing. "We can go dump together, and bring back ties and rails. Your dad'll be ready for 'em soon."

Jeff pulled the sprag from between the spokes of the wheel, stepped back, and seized the handrail as his car started to roll. The tunnel sloped gently toward the portal. With the great weight of the load and its well-greased undercarriage, the tram moved easily along the rails.

Had it been someone else pushing a car right behind him, Jeff might not have cared to take his own ahead. A load could easily get out of control and go careening through the tunnel to disaster. But Tony, the Mileses had learned, was reliable as well as efficient. Jeff liked him thoroughly.

They went through the portal into sunshine, with the water from the drainage ditch where it came out of the tunnel making a drowsy splash. Tony switched his car off onto a short sidetrack to stay until they could push Jeff's out to the edge and dump it.

Tony was of medium size, strongly and compactly built, lithe in his movements even when wearing the white rubber laced boots and bulky clothes of the miner.

Together they pushed Jeff's load across the level to the edge of the dump. Jeff swung the lockbar over and they tipped the hinged car body.

"Cheese," Jeff said, watching the waste rock spill down, "this is a far cry from pay dirt."

Tony flashed white teeth beneath his close-clipped black mustache. "Don't you tell Elfida that. We're hoping maybe we can be married by Christmas."

53

"But there's the cave-in at the fault to clean out and timber," said Jeff. "That's not even started yet. Then all the drilling and blasting and mucking on the other side."

"I know. But a month ago there was no truck driveway up from the road, no track laid, no tool house, no cabin for me. Look at the place now."

"The cabin," Jeff reminded him, "you built, after hours. Aren't you sinking a lot in this whole venture, Tony?"

"Sure," agreed Tony, "but it's my opportunity for a start. So Elfida and I won't have to live in a tenant house on some farm where I'd get only wages and we'd always be dependent."

They switched cars, and dumped Tony's load of muck.

"What if you can't get married by Christmas?" Jeff asked.

"Then," said Tony, "we'll make it later. Maybe June. I guess that's *mañana* philosophy, isn't it?"

"I don't know if Dad's capital will hold out until June," Jeff said. "He's pouring a lot of money into this."

"Yes, that's why I'm putting in work, since I have no money to invest. But I'm not worrying. I don't know anybody that needs less worrying about than John Miles."

They fastened the two cars together by the drawbar couplings and began loading crossties for the track from the storage pile.

"If the Mule Ear doesn't pay out," Jeff concluded, "at least you'll have tried."

"Now that makes sense," said Tony, "only to a gringo. Like your proverb, 'Better to have loved and lost than never to have loved at all.' Better, I think, to love and get married." He laughed again, companionably. He was only five years older than Jeff.

"Of course," said Jeff, "when you put a lot into something, you want it to turn out right. But what if it doesn't, even after you've done your best? "

Tony said: " Then you feel plenty bad, and no kidding yourself. You forget it as soon as you can, and go on from there. If we put some rails on top of this, we'll have all we can push."

From the stock pile they loaded a number of lengths of steel rail, each of which extended along both cars. Then they pushed the whole load back into the mine. They arrived near the present end of the track perspiring freely. The materials they unloaded in a side bay dug back in the right wall of the tunnel.

Jeff walked on to the end of the track, where Dad with pick and shovel was attacking the rubble accumulated on the tunnel floor. " For this," Jeff remarked, " you didn't need college training."

" We could use more help," Mr. Miles admitted, wiping his face with a handkerchief, " if we could get it. But a person has to put some labor into anything he expects to get much out of, I always say. How about taking this load out, Jeff, and letting us use both empties? "

" O.K.," said Jeff. " How much farther to that cozy little spot where the fault caved in? "

" Not much farther," Dad told him. " We should be at it by this time next week."

Taking the car out and returning to his location where he began again to shape the foot-wide, foot-deep drainage ditch, Jeff wished that he could take as steady a view of his affairs as Dad and Tony did of theirs. He had, he knew, put plenty into his school and band during the last month.

His days had been filled with the business of classes, climaxed by band period. Evenings he'd practiced. A full two hours of technical exercises and going over note by note

55

his part in every number in that thick band folio, shut away in his big room with only Perry to accompany him with mourning when the music was sad. After that came home-work — always.

Yes, he'd not spared the labor. But he seemed, as far as he could tell, to be advancing not at all. Oh, he had a uniform, and he'd appeared when the band appeared, and he knew the names of several kids. But he had not, really, any part in their doings. Hadn't acquired, certainly, any companion. And, it seemed sometimes, he had earned dislike by his very efforts to win a welcome.

The portal was blocked, so to speak, by Paul and Brick. Paul had resented him — for what reasons Jeff didn't know — from the first. And of course Brick followed Paul's lead like a trailer follows a truck, as in that first game after Jeff joined the band, when Lamont played at Garrison.

Carry your share of the load, Mr. Phillips had said.

Pondering that, Jeff had gone to work with the band. He knew his marching would be none too good, despite a quarter hour every evening when he stepped off in his room each maneuver Rosie had showed him. But playing was something else again. They planned to come out marching to the " National Emblem," turn cross file at the end of the first strain, and reverse in front of the stands as they began the second strain. That, Jeff remembered, was where the Garrison band had faltered the first time he and Ginny saw them. All week he'd practiced that passage until he had it letter-perfect.

When, in their half-time demonstration, they'd reached that critical spot, Jeff hit it with everything he had. The mass of the crowded stands threw the sound back. Deep-throated melody in the voice of the baritones and trombones. Wham! The cymbals crashed on an exclamation point.

Jeff stepped in Paul's tracks. Left face, left face again, and as he half stepped to the rear between files the clarinets were threading out their shrill tracery while the trumpets exulted above the staff. Jeff blew it out for all he was worth: "Oh, the monkey wrapped his tail around the flagpole!" He met the drums, Walt Terry on the bass swinging his two white padded sticks in spectacular arcs over his head from one side to the other, his face shining with excitement.

It was right! Jeff knew it was right. He could even feel the others knowing it was right! For the few moments while they finished the piece he had a feeling of connection as if by magnetic wires to every other player in the band, and they to him.

When they were once more settled in the stands, Mr. Phillips called generally, "Good going on 'National Emblem.'" Then, looking at him, added, "Nice work there, Jeff."

After the game Jeff drifted over to the Knot Inn confectionery. Inside, court was in session. Meaning, as Jeff phrased it silently, that the table where Paul sat was the center of goings and comings and greetings and conversation. Jeff got a malt at the soda bar and then, not caring to present himself as if for approval at the head boy's table, started on by. He was halted by Carol, who was sitting beside Paul.

"O Jeff! That was terrific, there in 'National Emblem'! We heard you hitting the melody and all the other parts seemed to fit right in." She gave him her prettiest smile. The black hair curled damply away from the white of her forehead where her uniform cap had been. Jeff felt a warmth of pleasure.

Before he could acknowledge her words, however, Paul said: "Yes, a baritone gives a lot of support to a band. I've noticed that with Mel for three years now. I hope Phillips

57

gets around to recognizing your work some of these days, Mel."

Mel, who was sitting at Paul's table that day, flushed quickly, and Carol's face colored too, despite the nod, wink, and grin that went with Paul's remark.

"I thought the whole baritone section came in strong today," Carol said lamely.

"Why, thanks, sporty!" chimed in Brick. "Thanks for keeping us in mind."

Jeff got out as quickly as he could — not, however, without hearing words trail after him. "Didn't finish his malt. . . . Must feel we don't appreciate . . ." Jeff closed the door on the rest of it.

Someday, he thought grimly, he was going to treat himself to relocating a few of Lassiter's teeth. But in a few moments he reached the realization that there was no future in that. Actually Brick amounted to nothing but a seconder to Paul's motions.

No, Paul set the pace, not only for Brick but for the whole school. By getting started wrong with Paul, in some unknown way, he had cut himself off from being accepted by anybody who was anybody.

That, Jeff reflected, had become only more clear as time went along. He thought it over again as he slogged away now in the Mule Ear tunnel, picking and shoveling at the mud without much heed either for it or for the down-squeezing masses of granite above him.

Not that there'd been any clash. It would have been easier if there had. Paul continued to flash his nod, wink, and grin whenever they met, and say, "Hiya, Miles." Only Paul's tone, somehow, always carried disdain, as if he spoke to someone who had borrowed a quarter and refused to pay it back. Brick, on the other hand, took to ignoring Jeff's existence. Mel never failed to nod, but the gesture held no meaning. Carol was pleasant but impersonal.

It all enraged Jeff. He'd never intended to do anything but show he'd carry his share of the load. There matters had stood ever since, with his having a part in the band's pieces, but no part in its fun and fellowship. Searching his mind for reasons, he came up with only one thing that made sense — Paul's eager-beaver crack.

So Jeff had tried being inconspicuous. No more leading out, he'd resolved. Then he'd get caught up in the swing of a Sousa march or a Strauss waltz and the first thing he knew he'd be playing away at top level, unmindful of anybody. He couldn't give such music, or a swell guy like Mr. Phillips, less than his best.

Some mud plopped at his feet, and Jeff came back to the present again and the realization that his car was full. He pushed it out and dumped it, got himself a drink. Dad and Tony came out of the tunnel just then.

"Eleven o'clock," Dad announced. "We'd better start for home if we're going to get cleaned up and make a football game in Parkville by two. See you Monday, Tony."

Jeff drove Dad and Mom over to Parkville for the game. Ginny was to come later as the guest of Betty Jean, with Mr. and Mrs. Hardesty, and another ninth-grader named Darlene York, who was also a friend of Betty Jean.

"Won't the Hardestys be crowded?" Jeff wondered.

"I checked with Mrs. Hardesty," said Mom. "Carol is going with some band youngsters who are taking a car."

He might have guessed, Jeff thought. Carol would go with Paul in Brick's convertible. Probably Sylvia Dodd, a blonde who played clarinet and whose dad was president of the bank, would be with Brick. Who's Who and Why of Garrison High, those four.

Dad chuckled. " Hardesty was saying, when I was in the hardware the other day, that he remains the innocent by-stander as much as possible. Since he's chairman of the Chamber of Commerce Music Committee, and Carol made first-chair first trumpet, he doesn't want to give any impression of throwing weight around."

Jeff drove at a brisk clip across the rolling country of the basin of Rio del Oro, but had to reduce speed over Bedroll Pass. It was easy and unspectacular as mountain passes go, but the highway curved and climbed, and then curved again as they dropped down the other side to Long's Park, of which Parkville was the chief town. The sixty miles from Garrison required nearly two hours' driving.

They were established in the stands, and Jeff was in the section reserved for band, warming his horn, when Who's Who and Why came in. The girls, Jeff thought, looked a trifle wind-blown, as if they'd ridden with the convertible's top down. Brick was evidently in high spirits as he took his place, though of course he gave Jeff no sign of recognition.

To Mel, Brick said, " Made it from Carol's house in an hour and fifteen minutes."

Mel shook his dark head. " It's an hour thirty-five if you hold full speed limits all the way. My dad and I clocked it last summer, one morning when we were going fishing early and there was no traffic on the road."

" Ah," Brick retorted happily, " there was a lot of traffic today that held us back."

Mel laughed with him, but said, " Some fine day you'll have to be scraped up with a shovel, you dope."

Mr. Phillips called out, " Take 'The Thunderer' to warm up."

At that juncture the Hardestys came in. Mr. Hardesty

60

stopped in the aisle while Mrs. Hardesty and the three girls sought seats.

"Brick," said Mr. Hardesty, "I want to see you and Paul and Carol and Sylvia. Since you're ready to play now, make it right after the half-time demonstration."

"Uh-oh," Brick muttered as Mr. Hardesty turned away, "what's biting Carol's old man?"

Evidently something was biting Mr. Hardesty, Jeff judged, because he stopped also to speak briefly to Carol, Paul, and Sylvia before he joined Mrs. Hardesty, and his tone had spelled trouble.

Curiosity rose even stronger in Jeff when, after the demonstration, he observed Mr. Hardesty talking with the four of them. Brick did a lot of talking too, gesticulating violently with his hands. Evidently Paul would have joined in, but Carol seemed to dissuade him, with a hand on his arm. All four were scarlet-faced and most unhappy-looking.

Brick seemed more furious even than he'd been when his marching place went to Jeff. He plopped into his seat, but Jeff could make nothing of the dark mutterings the redhead gave forth.

The Warriors came from behind to win the game, 9–7, in the last five minutes. With the frenzy of that excitement, Jeff would have forgotten the Brick incident, except that Brick and Paul kept slipping back and forth to confer with each other all during the second half.

When the game was finally over and Jeff joined his parents at the car, there were Ginny, Betty Jean, and Darlene York.

"We'll put your horn in the trunk," Dad drawled slowly, as he did when he meant more than he said. "The Hardestys need to make room for Carol and Paul on the return trip."

"For corn's —" Jeff began, but he stopped. Mr. Hardesty

was approaching them.

"The kids had plans," Mr. Hardesty said to Dad. "There's a place here in Parkville called The Spanish Kitchen that serves really excellent enchiladas. I hate to be a complete spoilsport, and I know Betty Jean will feel gypped if Carol gets to go and she doesn't. Would you folks care to join us for a plate of enchiladas?"

"Why . . ." said Dad, and looked across at Mom.

"I can't think of anything I'm hungrier for than enchiladas." Mom laughed, and the three girls jumped and squealed with delight.

During the short drive to The Spanish Kitchen, Betty Jean held forth excitedly about its food and atmosphere, so Jeff had no chance to learn more of what this was all about.

The Spanish Kitchen was a good-sized restaurant, gleaming with tile and white paint and bright Mexican pictures on the walls. But when Jeff saw the crowd, he stopped short.

The place was practically full of Garrison band kids, the same crowd that would have been in the Knot Inn after a game at home. The only difference was several tables of parents at one side. Jeff would have disappeared, but fast, if he could. He didn't care for any more such gatherings as the last he had attended at the Knot Inn.

As it was, Dad and Mom sat with Mr. and Mrs. Hardesty. The girls found a young sister of Bill Hayes to complete their table.

Bill, who played E-flat sax, said: "That leaves me odd man too. Let's take this small table, Miles." In silent gratitude, Jeff joined him.

The Mexican girl waitresses moved rapidly among the tables, saying: "Enchiladas? There will be a small wait."

Jeff prepared to open conversation with Bill Hayes, but before he could speak a shout came from the rear.

" Hey, gang! " It was Brick standing at the table where he sat with Paul and Carol and Sylvia. " Spirit of the occasion. Paul's going to give us ' A Feller I Know,' by Mary Austin. Get a load! "

" This'll be good," Bill whispered in the quiet.

Paul stood and gave all the assemblage his nod, wink, and grin. Then he began reciting: " Pedro Pablo Ignacio Juan Francisco García y Gabaldón . . ." Complete with action and sound effects.

Everybody in the place was under Paul's spell from the first. He could change in a second from a kid playing ball to a Mexican mother baking cookies to a conquistador marching across unknown wilderness. And back again without pausing for breath!

When he finished, there was a storm of applause.

" How about Creede? " shouted Brick.

" Yeah. Give us Creede! "

" Please, Paul! " The kids took it up.

Creede was a famous old mining camp, now almost a ghost town, and also the subject of a poem, Jeff recalled.

Paul's recitation proved to be a parody, a riot of the ridiculous. One instant he was a tinhorn gambler, a deadly snub-nosed revolver up his sleeve, and when he fired it went " Phht! Phht! " In the next breath he became a glamorous dancing girl, whose feet were killing her. The girls in the audience shrieked with appreciative delight. Cheese, Jeff thought, the guy's got 'em in the hollow of his hand!

By now Paul was a grizzled prospector; all the mines he'd discovered were duds. He'd spent his last nickel on a glass of beer, and a fly had drowned in the suds. The kids howled and rocked in their chairs. Then came a savage gun duel, " Pow-pow-pow! " and " Whup-whup-whup! " Even the grownups were shouting with laughter.

63

An absolute ovation burst forth at the close. Paul stood there, waving gaily, his charming nod, wink, and grin assuring each person in the room that the performance was all for him alone. Jeff had wondered, of late, how so arrogant a character as Paul had ever been elected head boy. Now he knew. He'd seen some student leaders, in several high schools, but never one with the wit, the pleasing manner, the complete crowd appeal of Paul Spencer.

Also, this was the fellow who had it in for Jeff Miles, a mystery now greater than ever, when Paul so plainly liked people, wanted friends, sought popularity. That realization plunged Jeff into gloom.

As they were finishing their food, Paul approached the table where the Miles and Hardesty parents sat. He looked straight at Jeff, then at Bill Hayes, said, " Hiya, Bill," and turned his back.

" Look, Mr. Hardesty." Never was a tone more winning. " Let's not be hasty about this thing, hunh? "

" I'm sorry, Paul," Mr. Hardesty said clearly. " Carol is simply grounded, permanently, from Brick's car. Is Sylvia going to come with us? "

" No, sir. She's sticking with Brick."

" I wish her father had come today."

Paul straightened abruptly; Jeff felt his staring down. " I hope," he muttered to Jeff in a furious undertone, " you managed to get in on it all, as usual! " He moved away.

" My gosh," said Bill Hayes, "what'd *you* do? "

To that Jeff had no answer.

After unlocking the car, Jeff handed the keys to his father. " Maybe you'd better drive," he said.

" Why? " asked Mr. Miles. " You're doing a safe, sane job."

" Boy," Betty Jean volunteered from the back seat, " did

64

Daddy ever blow his top about Brick's driving! We were on one of those long curves coming down off Bedroll Pass, in a regular line of cars with practically everybody in Garrison on their way to the game. And here Brick went tearing past at about seventy on the outside of the yellow line."

"A little farther on," Darlene added, "he met a car coming up, and if somebody hadn't slowed and let Brick back into line, there'd have been a mess."

Jeff remembered what Mel had said to Brick about having to be scraped up with a shovel some fine day.

"I'm glad we didn't start home right after the game," Dad shifted the subject. "The road's less crowded now. And isn't it a grand evening for driving?"

Later, at home, with the family gathered in the kitchen for a bowl of cereal and milk to supplement their semidinner of enchiladas, Virginia returned to the incident.

"Since Carol's not allowed to ride with Brick, Jeff, you ought to ask to take her to the next out-of-town game. You needn't try to let on you're not interested."

"That'd just fix me up dandy," Jeff retorted. "Paul's already sore at me, I guess because I heard Mr. Hardesty setting him down."

"Did he think you could help finding out," Ginny demanded, "when you had to bring us three girls home on that account?"

"I don't know," Jeff admitted. "I do know I'm not doing myself any good to keep running afoul of Paul all the time."

"Don't be a supercilious jerk. You talk like Paul was National Underwriters or somebody. Can't anybody be your friend without Paul Spencer's O.K.?"

"The way he rates around Garrison High," Jeff mused, "I'm not sure. I'm not sure."

CHAPTER 5

JEFF HAD no more than taken his place at the next band rehearsal when the second majorette approached.

"Mr. Phillips wants to see all you baritones in the hall."

Jeff rose and laid his horn on the chair. He hadn't the slightest notion what this might mean, but Mel and Brick were heading toward the door, and he followed.

Mr. Phillips, his dry voice unusually quiet, said: "I don't go for stalling. I'm putting Jeff on first chair. As of now."

There was a moment of swelling silence. Jeff couldn't catch up with his thoughts right away. He had heard of the custom among professional musicians of designating players in order of ability as first chair, second chair, and so on. He had not, however, given any consideration to whether that practice was followed here in the high school band.

Apparently Brick had. "So," the redhead blurted, "Carol's old man wasn't satisfied with the stink he raised at the game Saturday! He had to see I was knocked down."

"You can believe that if it makes you feel any better," Mr. Phillips cut in. "If you can stomach the truth, Jeff is a stronger player than either of you, and has been almost from the time he came in."

Mel asked, carefully steady, "Is that all, Mr. Phillips?"

He, Jeff realized, was the one who was really taking the jolt.

"No," said Mr. Phillips, "I want to say also that you're a good sport and a good bandsman, Mel. I appreciate it, and the school appreciates it."

"That," added Brick, "is why you're getting the ax, Mel."

Jeff was beginning to collect his wits. "Sir," he said, "could I ask a question?"

"Sir," answered Mr. Phillips, "you could."

Jeff realized his slip in speech, but he persisted. "Is it necessary to change? I mean, I can play the same in one chair as another, and I don't want to cause trouble."

Mr. Phillips drawled: "I wish I had a few more that made your kind of trouble. This band would go places. In my opinion, the change is necessary. You *don't* play the same in one chair as another. I've observed you, at times, holding in. Now it's your responsibility to play out and lead the section."

"Ha!" Brick said.

But Mel said, "Come on, let's get going." And, taking Brick's arm, he led the way back into the band room.

The bell had rung, Rosie was waiting with the attendance slip for Mr. Phillips' O.K., and Paul was directing the tune-up scale. He cut while the three baritones sought their places.

Jeff reached to take his horn from the chair that was now Brick's. As he did so, the chair tilted suddenly, and had he been an inch farther away, his euphonium would have dropped to the floor.

He straightened in anger, but then he realized that everyone in the room was watching them curiously. Through long years of experience, Jeff had developed an allergy to stares, and he suddenly felt ten feet tall and three wide. Too, he felt sorry for Mel. He sat down quickly to avoid calling more attention to Mel's demotion.

When he looked up, he met Paul's eyes glaring at him.

Then the head boy glanced down at Carol.

She, Jeff saw, was smiling at him, and she raised her clasped hands briefly in a gesture of congratulation.

All of a sudden it came to Jeff what had happened. He'd made first chair! Received an honor! He played that entire rehearsal with growing enthusiasm.

After rehearsal, several bandsmen stopped to say, " Congratulations." Henrietta Ralston, the tall, shy girl who served as librarian and played first-chair French horn, Walt Terry, Bill Hayes. Most of the band had left by the time Jeff got his horn cased and started out.

He went from the running track to the first-floor hall rapidly, planning what he would say when he announced the news at dinner.

" Outa the way of the big shot, y' goon! " rasped a voice. " Don't you know a first-chair musician when you see one? "

Jeff looked up to see Brick, squarely in his path, shouldering Mel aside. Paul was standing by. So! Jeff knew a sudden, savage pleasure. He set his horn down. " Meaning me? " he asked.

" Meaning you! " Brick admitted. " Want to make somep'n of it? "

" Sure," Jeff said, and laughed out of tension. He couldn't help it.

Lassiter lunged, swinging. Jeff shifted his feet, blocked with his elbows, rode with the rush to get his back to the wall. He'd take on the three of them one at a time, but long years ago he'd learned not to let himself be ganged. Learned it the hard way, the way a new kid in town learns it.

" Brick! Wait! " Paul cried sharply.

Jeff braced, half shoved and half cuffed, and threw Brick back. The redhead shucked his jacket violently, shaking off Paul's restraining hand. Jeff kept his guard up.

" Beeeef! Beeeef! " The bellow echoed along the corridor and feet thundered as lingering students swarmed to the excitement.

Brick set himself. Jeff waited, thinking, I hadn't intended it'd be this way at Garrison. Alone. Back to the wall. Like a coyote cornered in a little empty circle surrounded by a yapping, snapping pack. All so familiar, so sickeningly familiar, to a kid who'd been the new kid in so many, many towns.

Then the circle parted forcibly and there was Mr. Case, the teacher of solid geometry. Jeff hadn't thought about the geometry room being close by.

" Break it up! " Mr. Case ordered. " Break it up! You know better than to start a tussle in the halls, Lassiter, even if Miles is new. Now come on, both of you."

Jeff was sick. Sure, he could *tell* the principal, when they got to the office, that Brick started the thing. But the crowd was coming along. What chance would there be of making his word stick? Mr. Case had his hands under one of his elbows and one of Brick's, walking between them.

" When you want to fight in this school," the teacher remarked, " you do it right. In the gym, with gloves and a referee."

Jeff swallowed his astonishment. This was one wrinkle he'd not come across before. But as the idea sank in, his heart began to pound with anticipation. Here was a break such as he'd never dreamed of!

In a gym, with ring rules enforced by a referee, he'd have a chance. This wouldn't be a gang-up in a back alley. Jeff knew all the angles to this game. His knowledge dated back to when he was seven, and the town was Dewport. Or Norville. He'd forgotten.

But anyway, when he'd finally got healed up after that

69

one, his dad took over and provided boxing instruction at the Y.M.C.A., or from whatever teacher could be had wherever they were living. He'd bought gloves and rigged punching bags. Boxing became Jeff's hobby, his pride, and his chief interest until his horn came along. Even then there'd been plenty of times . . . Jeff had become a veteran at the fight game before his voice started to change.

Now Mr. Case pushed into the locker room. The gym teacher, who was also football coach, was supervising the football team as the fellows suited up for practice.

"Difference of opinion here, Coach," said Mr. Case.

"Thanks, Mr. Case." The big man looked them over a moment. "You fellows want to get this out of your systems now?"

"Now or any time he's got the nerve!" Brick blared. "Just so's I get the pleasure of taking him down off his high horse."

"Now's good." Jeff wasted no breath on bluster. Blatting throws no punches.

The coach said casually: "Get in your gym suits. I'll bring the gloves. Sullivan, see that mats are placed for a ring. Any of you football men I catch on the gym floor with cleats will be sorry."

Jeff turned to his gym locker and got out his shorts and sneakers. All this to-do made the whole business seem somehow a trifle silly, took away the satisfaction of striking out in a sudden burst of feeling and gave the affair a calculating-machine quality. The policy surely must tend to discourage fights in the school.

And with the twelve-ounce gloves the coach put on him, it would be about as deadly as a pillow fight!

But out on the gym floor, standing on a corner of the square of mats, Jeff again felt his aloneness. Hemmed in by a solid mass of faces! They wanted sport, and a strange kid makes the best game. Nobody feels it if a guy he doesn't know . . .

Jeff forced his attention back to Brick in the opposite corner. Lassiter was an inch or so shorter, but much heavier and better muscled than Jeff had expected him to be. Paul stood talking to Brick earnestly. Advice, no doubt. If Spencer was so full of ideas, why didn't he do the fighting himself?

The coach called Brick and Jeff to center. "Four rounds of two minutes each," he announced. "That's as far as I allow these things to go, even though you both passed the physical for gym work. I'll referee and enforce regular ring rules." The coach stepped back and looked at his watch. "O.K.," he said.

Brick went up on his toes, left leading, right cocked, and feinted for an opening. Plainly he knew some basics of boxing and intended to make a spectacle for the crowd of how he handled the newcomer.

Jeff dropped the ponderous gloves to his sides, flexed his knees, and stuck his chin forward in the style of the old-time champ Tommy Ryan.

Brick took the bait and swung a whistling right. Jeff lunged inside the right and drove his own left short and hard just above the belt.

The breath went out of Brick with a *whuf!* and he dropped back two steps. Jeff leaped after him, swinging with both hands. Brick gave ground again. With six-ounce gloves, Jeff was sure he would have done some damage. With these sofa cushions —

"You want a fight?" he croaked, as Brick backed again.

Brick rushed. Jeff met him head on and they slugged, toe to toe. A full-throated roar went up from the crowd.

A smash caught Jeff alongside the head. Another exploded

71

on his collarbone. He shook his head to clear the ringing in his ears and lashed out, driving his punches from the waist.

Somewhere a voice said, " Time! " Then the coach's hands pulled them apart.

Jeff plodded to his corner, deliberately taking it easy to get full advantage of the break for restoring his wind and his strength. Lassiter was no pushover.

But Jeff thought he was getting the better of it. He looked at the crowd from the corner of an eye. They were shifting their feet and exchanging brittle comments. They'd expected a wild-swinging brawl and were getting a good amateur bout.

The coach handed Jeff a towel. " You're not new at this? " " No, sir." Jeff didn't try to explain.

" Time."

Lassiter came out in a deep crouch, head hunched between his shoulders, fists far out in front. Jeff let fly two fast hooks.

He missed and found himself jarred and shaken. Then he realized Lassiter had caught him, coming in, with smashes to the body.

Jeff sparred on the defensive. But he couldn't reach Brick and he couldn't dodge that body punishment. The pillowy gloves did no real injury, but enough of this could weaken a person, eventually drop him. The crowd began to shout.

" Take him, Lassiter! "

" Cool him, Brick! "

Jeff couldn't clear his head. It seemed two hours before the coach said, " Time! "

Jeff went to his corner and picked up his towel. The football men were yelling. Jeff's middle had begun to ache. He looked across at Lassiter.

Brick was sitting on one of Paul's knees, panting. Somebody else was wiping the redhead's face. In a way, it was the alley again. Friends to help a friend; nobody to help the new kid. The unfairness of it cleared Jeff's head. And suddenly he remembered, out of his boxing lessons, what to do with a croucher.

As they came to the center again, Jeff sent out a left lead. Lassiter swung for the body. Jeff brought up his right in an uppercut from below his knees full into Brick's face.

Lassiter straightened and staggered. Jeff plunged after him, driving him across the ring of mats, slashing furiously with both hands. A startled roar reached his ears. He struck as fast as he could work his arms.

But Lassiter didn't go down, and the round ended with them slugging toe to toe again.

Jeff knew he had made a mistake. He'd been too eager and too many of his blows had gone wild.

" Time! " said the coach.

Lassiter tried crouching once more, and once more Jeff broke it up. Then Brick tried to spar, but counterpunching was Jeff's style. He picked his spots and drove his punches home.

The crowd had gone silent. The thud of Jeff's gloves was loud, almost echoing. Brick lashed out desperately, and missed. Brick's head began to snap on his neck at every merciless jolt as the redhead struggled to stay on his feet.

" Time! " said the coach. " That does it."

Lassiter dropped his gloves and stumbled away toward a corner. The wrong corner. Paul rushed out and seized him.

Jeff turned to the coach. " If we could have one more round . . ."

The coach grinned. " Don't be bloodthirsty." He removed Jeff's gloves.

Jeff started toward the locker room. The students parted and let him through.

Something caused him to look up as he went. Leaning over the iron railing of the running track above was Mr. Phillips. Jeff couldn't tell for sure, in the uncertain light, but he thought the lean features of the conductor wore that dry grin.

Jeff was changing his shoes in the locker room when Brick came in, still stumbling, with Paul and Sullivan, the football captain.

When he'd finished knotting a shoelace, Jeff walked over. "I guess it's customary to shake hands," he offered, and extended his own.

Brick snarled, "Nuts to that noise!"

Jeff got his horn and went home, not seeing at all the far-flung ribbon of silver fire that rimmed the Continental Divide with sunset, not noticing the crisp tang of the autumn air.

There was high excitement around the Miles dinner table that evening. Dad was inclined toward an absent-minded little grin, while Mom cluck-clucked over Jeff's bumps and bruises. Actually, he had incurred no damage that wouldn't be restored by a soaking hot bath and a good night's sleep.

"I think the important thing," Ginny declared, "is that Jeff got first-chair baritone. Is everybody forgetting that?"

"You're right, Ginny," Dad agreed. "That is the important thing. I foresee a lot more developments as a result of that."

"What else can happen to me?" Jeff wanted to know.

"That's hard to say," Dad answered. "Only keep yourself braced. You didn't just beat this fellow; you beat him in front of the entire football squad."

"You want him to win when he fights, don't you?" demanded Ginny.

"Of course," Dad nodded. "Only don't expect that now

74

all will be forgotten and forgiven, as is the case usually among younger boys. You're set up now in a conspicuous position, both by becoming first-chair baritone and by winning this fight. That you'll have more than one occasion to prove yourself is my guess."

"I've got some news too," said Ginny, who had reached her limit of conversation on one subject. "Betty Jean and I are going to work up a puppet play to present in Latin class. The teacher said we could, instead of a report, and it'll be a lot more fun."

"Why, that's fine, Ginny!" said Dad. "If you need any help fixing up your stage, let me know."

"And I'll have the scrap bag ready for costumes," Mom offered.

Jeff said, "If you want any gladiators, see me."

He skipped horn practice that night, out of weariness, though luckily his face had escaped any injury that would interfere with his playing. He didn't know what to expect as a result of all that had happened today, but at least he had a hunch he would no longer be simply ignored.

His hunch was right. Next morning as he walked along the hall, curious stares followed him. He heard a sentence, "Shoulda been in gym with us yesterday afternoon."

As he moved into the corridor traffic after first period, he encountered Brick, along with Paul and a close knot of other cronies. Brick's face was a little discolored.

Without sign of recognition, Brick turned to enter a classroom. A small freshman piped up humorously: "Watch the door, Lassiter. Don't run into it in the dark."

"Shut your mouth!" Brick snarled into the ripple of laughter.

Jeff walked on through thick silence.

"Miles."

Jeff stopped and waited for Paul to overtake him. For certain, he thought grimly, things had changed. Never before had Paul sought him out.

Paul said, "Since all this has come up, and I was the one that got you into band, I ought to give you some advice."

You got me into band, Jeff thought in amazement.

"You'd be smart to resign first chair," Paul stated.

Jeff said, "I don't get it."

"Mel is well known, popular, has a long record of service to the organization," Paul explained in a tone of great patience. "The kids resent your crowding him out."

"I didn't," Jeff began, and stopped. He felt, without knowing why, that this conversation was out of place. Finally he asked, "So what?"

"So to get on the good side of the regular people, you ought to resign."

"I'll quit band first!" Jeff said hotly.

"That's up to you," returned Paul. "There's a petition starting around asking Phillips to put Mel back in first chair. I thought if you knew that, you could get to Phillips first."

"Who got up this petition?" Jeff demanded.

Paul shrugged. "A petition is always just one of those things. Popular demand. I've had a lot of experience with that stuff, holding offices."

"Somebody has to start 'em," Jeff persisted. "I didn't think Mel was that kind of guy."

"As I said, he has lots of friends. If you want time to think it over, I can keep the petition from being presented to Phillips until after school Friday."

"Don't trouble yourself!" Jeff spun on his heel and walked away.

But he was sick at heart. Even a place he had earned, he

couldn't keep in this town. Not, at least, without the approval of Paul Spencer. The more he thought about it, and he could think of little else after that, the surer he was that the petition had been started by none other than Paul. Paul had had a lot of experience with petitions. And it was the sort of slick operation that would be like Paul.

At seventh hour there was not the usual lighthearted din. A few tootlings, but no gaiety. Jeff took the first chair in the baritone section as casually as he could. Mel sat down in second. Brick was nowhere in sight.

At the bell, Rosie announced the absentees, and then looked inquiringly at Mr. Phillips.

"Brick is excused from band the rest of this week," Mr. Phillips said. His tone was expressionless.

The playing was ragged. Mr. Phillips at first displayed his usual patience under a layer of tartness. "Now, kids, that was very chop suey." But toward the end his words became sharp and his patience evidently exhausted.

After the usual forty minutes they went out to march. Their marching was no better than their playing, and Rosie and Peggy were soon looking very unhappy. A remark that Mr. Phillips had made strayed into Jeff's mind: "The one thing a band has to be is together."

School had been out ten minutes when they heard a loud "Bee-eep!" A maroon convertible shot down the street, swerved and slowed as it neared them. It was piled with guys, no less than eight, hanging all over it.

"Hup! Hup! Hup!"

"Slog it, you dog faces!"

"Whaddya do in the in-fan-tree? Ya march! *March!* MARCH!"

Suddenly the car picked up speed and disappeared around the corner with a squeal of protesting rubber. Mr. Phillips said no word but Jeff, only two paces away from where the director marched at the right of the band, saw the back of his neck become violently red.

When, fifteen minutes later, the convertible appeared again, Mr. Phillips gave a smothered exclamation and started for the curb. Paul immediately broke ranks and stepped over to speak to him.

Jeff heard, as he marched on past, "Take it easy, maestro, I'll get to him tonight." By that time the convertible was gone.

If that was a bad day, however, the next three were infinitely worse for Jeff. Paul's petition went the rounds. Not that Jeff was supposed to know, but glimpses of kids writing on a paper, and then whisking the paper out of sight when they saw him, and the half-unfriendly, half-shame-faced way kids averted their eyes when they met him all added up. Even Carol did not offer her usual smile.

It was, Jeff thought, the dirtiest thing that had ever been done to him in any school. He could almost have developed a liking for Brick by contrast. Brick threw his opposition squarely in your teeth, and then stood up to face you. This, there was no way to meet. And somehow he could not bring himself to talk of it at home.

He was tempted to throw the whole thing over. Quit band. But sheer stubbornness kept him going to his assigned place.

Saturday morning he entered the Mule Ear Mine with vast relief. Here he could get his mind off what must have gone on yesterday afternoon after school when that paper was presented to Mr. Phillips. And in the mine he could work off his helpless fury in violence with pick and shovel on unfeeling rock.

Dad and Tony were laboring now at the tumbled mass

of the caved-in fault zone. The rock and the mud had to be dug out for the width and height of a good haulage way, and timbers and lagging were used to keep more of the stuff from sliding into the cleared space.

There was plenty of outlet for Jeff's energy. The mud, which got wetter as they worked farther back in the mine, had by now become sloppy enough to pour. Every time he scooped up a shovelful, it seemed to him that twice as much plopped into its place.

"I don't like the looks of the water situation," Dad observed as they went toward the portal to eat their lunches in Tony's cabin. "I suspect the workings beyond the fault may have filled up with water during the years. The cave-in amounts to a perfect dam."

"It may drain over Sunday," said Tony, always optimistic. "It's seeping through fast. You notice the drainage ditch is running practically full all the time now."

"That helps," Dad agreed. "Fortunately the workings on the other side are pretty much on this same level. I'd not care to hang around long if that much water started coming through suddenly under pressure of a lot of gravity."

"It is not a day for wet feet," laughed Tony. Winter had made its beginning in high country. They came out to a day of dull gray cast, with lowering clouds that brought occasional squalls of snow. A chill wind whimpered down the sweep of Hoodoo Gulch.

After lunch Dad said: "Tony and I will frame another set of timbers and bring them in, Jeff, if you want to go ahead and shovel off the floor. But I wouldn't fool with the face of the slide very much while you're by yourself. We're not sure how thick it may still be, nor how much water's on the other side."

So Jeff hiked back along the track and at the slide began

again the endless spooning of slush into an ore car. He was doing rather well until he bumped his head. He looked up. The knock hadn't really hurt because of his metal hat but a long fragment of rock protruded from the slide at exactly the height and angle to be in his way in this confined space.

He considered prying the rock out, but Dad had said not to disturb the slide. Jeff went ahead, with care to avoid the obstacle. Nevertheless he bumped it again.

At the third bang Jeff gave an angry exclamation. The blamed thing was getting to be a nuisance. He seized the pick, drove the blade into the mass above the rock, and pried up on the handle. The offending chunk slid forth down the face of the slide. Jeff stepped back quickly to get his feet out of the way.

A burbling sound caused him to look up. And to stare.

From where the rock had been a stream of muddy water was spouting forth, the size of a fire hose. In the seconds while Jeff stared in dismay, the dirt and rock crumbled around it and the stream grew in size. He'd better get Dad.

His boots made splashing sounds. He looked down. A thin layer of water covered the floor of the tunnel for its whole width. He looked back. In the light of the Wolf lamp the stream was foaming out a dirty yellow, and the slide was caving down with it visibly and — Corn's sake!

Jeff whirled and started to run down the middle of the mine track.

With the speed of his motion, the carbide flame of his lamp blew out. He was plunged abruptly into solid, directionless black. He became aware of sound filling the tunnel, a splashing and a sort of grinding hiss.

His heart jolting against his ribs, he groped to his left until he touched the rock wall of the tunnel. In spite of shaking fingers he managed to get his lamp going again.

In its light he saw the drainage ditch overflow and water begin to swirl against the track bed. Every nerve in him howled to make a dash for it at full speed. But he forced himself to a jog trot, for fear of blowing out his lamp if he ran.

Disjointed thoughts reeled through his mind. The dread of all miners was being trapped underground. No day for wet feet! The whole tunnel was less than a thousand feet long, but it seemed like a thousand miles. Dad and Tony might be coming —

Jeff tried to shout. He was out of breath. Not going so fast, but — He gasped for air and began calling hoarsely as he went: " Go back! Flood! Go back! Flood! "

He was still shouting as he stumbled through the portal: " Go back! Flood! " Dad and Tony ran toward him.

" What on earth? " Dad demanded.

Jeff could only stand, his chest heaving like that of an emotional actress in a bad movie. " I — I picked a rock out of the slide," he gasped. He had no need to explain further.

The splashing of the drainage ditch at the portal suddenly grew in volume. While they watched, it filled and spread and rose until a muddy stream was rolling out, covering the bottom of the opening from side to side, sloshing over the tops of the rails in the track.

Jeff realized he was shaking in every muscle. He looked down at his hand and began to laugh unsteadily.

" Look! I carried my pick all the way out and never knew I had it till just now."

" Throw it down anywhere," Dad said soberly. " You won't be needing it again today. None of us will get into the Mule Ear again until after the flooding is over."

He led the way toward Tony's cabin. They went in and built up the fire.

CHAPTER 6

"I F I HADN'T loosened that blamed rock," Jeff said gloomily.

"Probably I would have," Dad finished, "when I got there. The main thing is, you got out all right."

"It wasn't your fault the supercilious water was backed up." Ginny added further comfort.

The whole family were on their way, early Sunday morning, to find out the extent of the damage at the Mule Ear. It was sharp winter along the bottom of the gulch.

They found Tony on the flat in front of the portal, wielding a shovel. Several gullies, of sizes to require jumping across, had been washed in the level surface, and Tony was filling them in. Water was coming from the portal only in a single stream at one side of the track now, but the floor of the tunnel as far back as they could see was heaped and smeared with oozing yellowish silt. Perry took a few questioning sniffs at the situation and promptly elected to go with Mom and Ginny into the cabin. Showing, Jeff thought, considerable wisdom.

It was a disheartening mess. They brought an ore car up to the edge of it and began scraping and scooping. Slow, hard, dirty work! The mud was too thick to flow and too thin to stay put. It had drifted in sweeps and riffles, sometimes deep over the rails, sometimes only enough to clog the drainage ditch.

Before they had worked their way back very far, they began to find fragments of rock in the mess. The water, washing up a foot or more higher than usual, had dislodged chunks from the tunnel walls. One sizable piece of the granite had rolled onto the track.

"This'll take months to clean up," Jeff predicted.

"Oh, no," said Dad. "That would mean as much to do as when we started. We can't be that bad off."

"After all," Tony pointed out, "we had no track then. Now it's laid clear up into the face of the tunnel."

"Then how much have I set you back?" asked Jeff.

"I don't know," Dad answered. "But you didn't set us back. As much water as there was had to go somewhere, sometime."

"We couldn't have carried it out in pails," declared Tony. "It ran nearly all night."

Jeff needed their reassurance. "I wonder what happened back there at the fault?"

"I can wait till we get there to find out," grinned Tony. "It'll wait for us, whatever's happened." He removed the sprag from the car wheel and began to shoulder the car forward a few feet for more convenient loading.

"Hold it, Tony!" Dad exclaimed.

But he was too late. One wheel of the car slipped off inside the rail and came down on the ties with a thud.

"Well, what caused that?" Jeff demanded.

"Track spread. The ties aren't held firmly by this soft mud, and we're on a turn here. When the force of the car pushed against the rail, the ties started to skid. It put some unusual stresses on the rails and maybe loosened some spikes. Anyhow, the rails were shoved too far apart."

"Corn's sake! Things get no better fast."

"A certain amount of spread track was to be expected,"

83

Dad observed, undismayed. "When the drainage has gone on a little longer, we can tamp in the ties again in soft places. Meanwhile, how would you like to prowl back and see what the worst is? That car won't go away while we're gone."

They walked back through the tunnel. It was no better, and not much worse, than the part they had seen. In some places rock loosened by the water had caused more rock higher up to give way and chunks of stone were strewed across the track, but that looked worse than it actually was.

At the fault zone the new timbering had stayed in place, which was the best news they could have had. Everything at the end of the timbered space was a tumbled mass, but that, as Dad remarked, was no different from what it had been.

"I thought there'd be a hole through to the other side," said Jeff.

"Probably more rock and dirt caved down than was washed out," Dad guessed. "Water will be backing in there again, but it will not have time to get nearly so deep now, and we can let it out gradually when we get to it. Think it'll be two weeks, Tony?"

"At least ten days," Tony nodded.

"If we never have any worse luck," concluded Dad, "we'll not complain."

Anyway, they knew the worst about the Mule Ear, Jeff reflected next day. Which was more than he knew about his own fate in band. With his concern over the mine, the petition to unseat him from first chair had receded from his thinking.

Now the day had to be waited out until seventh hour, when Mr. Phillips would no doubt take the matter up. Jeff couldn't keep his mind on his classwork. First he'd decide that, should he be taken off first chair, he'd quit. Then he decided that would seem like poor sportsmanship. He'd stick it out. He hadn't fully realized until he came up against losing it how much that first chair meant to him.

The hours did finally tick away, and Jeff walked slowly toward the band room. There everything appeared as usual. Even Brick was back, his usual noisy self. Rosie named the absentees. Paul was standing by to lead the warm-up scale, but he looked expectantly at Mr. Phillips.

Mr. Phillips placed a chair beside the podium. " Sit here for now, Paul," he said, and mounted the platform himself. " Instruments down. I want to talk."

Paul sat down, a gleam in his eyes. Jeff glued his attention to the engraving on his horn bell.

Mr. Phillips picked up two sheets of paper from the stand. " First thing, I have here a petition asking me to put a certain player on first chair of his section." He paused. " I guess I haven't made it clear about positions."

No one seemed to breathe.

" It's like this: Each of you has an instrument, either your own or one of the school's. You can practice all you want to. Get as good as you can. When you play better than anybody else in your section, I'll move you to first chair. There's no other way to get there! Is that clear? "

The sudden stinging lash of his words seemed to leave the room frozen.

" So much," said Mr. Phillips, " for the petition." He tore it methodically to bits, the small ripping sounds echoing in the silence.

Jeff thought he would burst. He thought — he didn't know what he thought!

" And *another* thing. There've been times this year when

85

your playing's been pretty near right. I've almost not been ashamed to be seen with you in public. In other words, you've been good — blamed good. Shall I go on, or do you want to brood awhile?

"Every year the Colorado Music Educators hold a mid-winter conference. I'm included, in spite of how dignified it sounds. One of the things we do is arrange for the regional music festivals held in the spring. At the festivals high school musicians get together for a big jamboree and play for ratings."

Somebody ventured, "Is that the whing-ding Paul and Carol attended at Murdock last year?"

"Yes. They went as soloists, and we had that flute trio whose members graduated. I haven't taken the whole band for some time. Five years ago we had an outstanding group, practically all seniors. You could be even better, by spring."

"You mean you might take the whole band again?"

"Better than that," returned Mr. Phillips. "I mean we might ask for the festival here this year. It's something we've never done."

"Wow!" and "Hey! Hey!" were the answers to that.

Carol exclaimed: "Oh, that would be super! It's really a big thing, with loads of visitors from all the neighboring schools, and social events, and everything!"

"Eats?" asked Dick, the oboe.

A whole assortment of cracks were fired back at him for that. This, Jeff thought, was like the playfulness of the day he'd joined the band. The strain and resentment of a few minutes before had been cast aside, somehow.

Presently Walt Terry called out, "We wouldn't get a trip if the festival was here."

"Squirrel food!" spoke up Brick. "I'll run you over to Murdock any afternoon if you're spoiling for a trip."

"The Music Educators select only towns where there's a really live band," Mr. Phillips said. "It takes enormous work to make all the arrangements and carry them out."

"O.K.," said Walt. "Anything to prove we're alive."

"How does the head of the student body feel about it?" asked Mr. Phillips.

Amidst the rapid developments, Jeff had almost forgotten Paul. Now he saw Paul look up in surprise.

"Why, it's all right, I guess. Sure."

"This seems to be Garrison High's year," Mr. Phillips stated. "Football team hasn't lost a game yet. Clubs doing well. Newspaper especially good. I can't remember a year when we had as many successful activities or better school spirit. Some folks say it's due to outstanding leadership." He smiled at Paul. "The band ought to do its part."

"Gosh, maestro!" Paul stuttered. "I think — I mean — Well, how about it, gang? You want to take hold of this?" He was on his feet suddenly, fairly beaming, the famous Spencer nod, wink, and grin flashing wide.

A full-throated "YES!" rose in chorus to answer him.

The enthusiasm grew. The festivals came the first week of May when the numerous orchards around Garrison would be in bloom. They would need money to entertain the visitors. The support of the whole town would be necessary. Why couldn't they put on a concert to raise money? Why not call it the Blossom Festival? The Chamber of Commerce would help, wouldn't it? The ideas came thick and fast, if at random.

Finally Mr. Phillips said, "Look, we have a game Saturday, and it's time for marching practice."

They drifted out to the recreation field, everybody talking. A suggestion had been forming in Jeff's mind, and at length he was so caught up in the spirit that he sought out Paul.

"You know," he said, "we might be able to get the town behind us by putting on a parade shortly before the festival. Invite the school clubs and organizations to enter floats or other displays to sell the idea that this is a big thing for Garrison."

Paul had been holding forth to a group that included Carol, Mel, Brick, and others. Now his face froze.

"That sounds like a grand idea!" was Carol's instant reaction.

"Why?" Paul asked. "The Chamber of Commerce can get the town's support. Sounds like a lot of extra work for nothing to me."

Jeff stared. "It was only a suggestion," he said shortly.

Paul snapped back: "You've won your point for the day! Do you have to elbow in on everything somebody else is doing?"

At that moment Rosie's whistle called them to formation. Jeff turned and stalked to his place.

He thought of the words, "Anything you say may be used against you." Anything you did too! Every move he made, Paul twisted to put him in the wrong! If ever he got a chance to even things . . .

He marched off some of his pent-up feelings, enough to remember that he *was* still first chair. A guy couldn't have everything. But that petition — the thing still stuck in his throat.

Now that the threat of it was past, however, he found he could at least talk of it. At dinner he told the family, describing dramatically how Mr. Phillips had torn the fateful paper to bits.

"Tore it up!" Ginny exploded. "I'd think he'd tear that supercilious Paul Spencer up! Why, I never heard of such a thing. A teacher letting kids get by with — "

Dad interposed: "I don't see that anybody got by with anything. It seems to me Mr. Phillips handled a pretty explosive situation with remarkable skill. In fact, the more I hear of Mr. Phillips, the more I'm impressed with the man."

Mom nodded, but Ginny smoldered. "I bet at Washington High a kid that'd pull a stunt like that would have been expelled."

"Maybe," said Mom. "I admit that at first Mr. Phillips sounded awfully free and easy to me, almost as if he were one of the youngsters."

"He's not, though," Jeff defended. "I don't know how to explain it exactly. He never gives a kid the brush-off, the way some adults do, and yet you wouldn't believe the work he gets out of most of 'em."

"I think you've said it," Dad nodded. "His work is creative. The players have to express themselves to bring out the feeling in the music. They couldn't do that if they were held down rigidly to showing great deference to a dictatorial director."

"As you say," Mom agreed, "he certainly dealt with this petition well. He might have thrown a scare into the youngsters that would have subdued them for months. Instead, he disposed of it quickly and turned their attention at once to something constructive in this music festival. I wish all high school band members might be so fortunate in a leader."

"I suppose that's impossible," mused Dad, "but there must be a good many who are highly skilled or there wouldn't be so many successful bands in the country and so many students who find the band the finest thing in their high school experience."

As Jeff set up for practice in his room after dinner, he

pondered that. Band was surely not all sweetness and light in his own experience, and yet he'd have to admit it was the one thing in school he'd most hate to be out of. Whatever that meant.

The doorbell rang about then. There were juvenile voices in the hall, and he heard Ginny's door open and shut. Betty Jean, no doubt, had come over to work on the puppet show.

It must have been about nine o'clock when the doorbell rang again. A clear voice floated up the stairs.

"Hello, Mrs. Miles. Do you have a stray youngster in the house?" It was Carol. "I thought maybe Betty Jean was jittery about coming home in the dark."

Jeff hustled down the stairs in the wake of the younger girls. Carol was wearing a thick sweater of white wool, with a ruff collar that brought out the soft contours of her face and the vivid color of her hair and eyes.

"Hi," said Jeff. "I scare spooks so they run away screaming. Especially on dark nights."

"Why, thank you, Jeff. We didn't mean to make a bother."

Jeff thought, Bother! Ha! He took his jacket from the hat tree. Virginia and Betty Jean had gone on ahead. As Jeff and Carol came down the steps, the girls jumped from the shadows, squealing and giggling.

"The Blossom Festival seems to have put the band on its feet," Jeff offered as they started up the hill.

"I thought your idea for a parade was a good one," returned the girl, and Jeff realized he had slipped in his choice of topics. About the last thing in the world he wanted to discuss with her was his feud with Paul. They stopped in front of her house, and Carol sat down on the low stone wall that prevented the Hardesty yard from sliding down the hill onto the sidewalk. She indicated a place for him beside her.

He sat down. A thought crossed his mind. If Paul should chance to come past just now!

"I'm sorry you and Paul aren't getting along," said Carol, and Jeff started. The girl must be psychic! "Personally, I think a lot of us owe you an apology for that petition."

Jeff scuffed his feet uncomfortably and muttered, "Aw, that's all right." He knew immediately that it was a lame thing to say.

"I'm furious at myself for signing it. I don't know if you can understand what happened." Carol paused as if to choose her words. "Everybody likes Paul a lot."

"Not quite everybody," Jeff said wryly, and felt that he was doing better. Her directness was still disconcerting.

"He's done a great deal for the school," she continued. "He has a way, too, of getting others to do almost better than their best. That's partly why Garrison High is having such an unusually good year."

She spoke, Jeff thought, as if she were leading up to something. He wondered what.

"Paul intends to be an outstanding head boy. When he was elected last spring, he had more votes than all the other candidates put together."

"I know he's very popular," Jeff nodded.

"One reason for his popularity is his loyalty. He always tries to help out anybody that's a supporter of his. So when Mel got demoted — well, he set out to cheer up a friend. I don't think any of us realized at the time how you — "

"Boo!" Ginny and Betty Jean sprang shouting from behind a tree and went into gales of laughter at the start they gave Jeff and Carol.

"Hey," Jeff said. "I'm supposed to be looking out for you two. Where have you been?" He was relieved to have this conversation interrupted.

"Oh, we circled the block while we had you to protect us," the youngsters chortled gleefully.

Later, after Carol and Betty Jean had gone in and he had returned home with Ginny, Jeff couldn't figure out any very good reason why Carol should have told him what she had. But she had been friendly, and he found himself a lot less inclined to feel that most of the kids in Garrison High were against him. They wouldn't know, he guessed, what it was like to be an outsider.

With a new challenge before them, the band settled down to serious work. Every rehearsal was crowded with drill, and with the endless going over and over of every passage, every phrase, section by section, part by part. It was the beginning of an extended grind, they knew, and they would not get their final satisfaction from it until next spring when they played at the Blossom Festival.

A money-raising concert was to be held in December. Then it was announced (nod, wink, and grin) that the student council had voted to get behind the band and was setting aside an assembly to present the festival plan to the student body.

"The council thought we should put on a novelty program," Rosie announced, "and between numbers we'll do our selling job. Paul will be M. C. and explain the musical ratings — general facts about the festival. Carol will give a preview of the social events. Walt will talk about the concert and how we have to have the money to put the festival over. And Jeff, we want you to tell 'em your plan for a parade with all the clubs and organizations having floats and things."

Jeff almost fell off his chair.

"Then Paul will wind it up with an appeal to buy tickets to the concert," Rosie went on matter-of-factly.

It would have been interesting, Jeff thought, to know in detail what went on at that council meeting. Had Paul opposed asking him to speak in assembly? Or had he thought it a good way of letting an upstart find out how little he amounted to in the eyes of the student body?

Jeff went to work on his talk with an intensity that would have astounded his English teacher. For days he thought of little else except by necessity. He tried out the talk on the family, rewrote it, and tried again.

Finally Dad said: "I think you're being too serious about it, Jeff. After all, the fate of nations doesn't hang on this parade."

"I think Dad's hit the point," Mom agreed. "It would be more appealing if it sounded more like lots of fun to do."

"And cut those supercilious wisecracks," admonished Virginia. "Paul Spencer does enough gagging and mugging without you —"

"My cherished chum!" Jeff grinned.

So on the day of the assembly, he had a brisk talk prepared in which he suggested a few possibilities for organizations to do some amusing things, get some favorable publicity for themselves, and have a good time in the doing. As a close, he would say he hoped they'd discuss it in meetings and let Paul know if they wanted to get in on the fun.

He had his talk memorized, and looked forward to the experience with some confidence as well as enthusiasm. But when the band gathered on the stage before the assembly and he looked out over those rows and rows of empty seats, clear up into the balcony where the seniors would sit, he felt suddenly as if he'd had no breakfast, and as they tuned up he had no notion whether he was playing B or G.

He heard Brick mutter to Mel: " I suppose the big wheel on your left is ready to roll. Lay-'em-in-the-aisles Miles! "

Jeff went hot and cold. It was an unusual day, recently, when Brick didn't mess up the baritone part at least once. He simply hadn't been practicing, Jeff was sure. Even this morning Mr. Phillips spent some time checking Brick's tuning slide, for he was flat in pitch again, meaning he hadn't been keeping his lip in shape.

Then the assembly bell rang, and Mr. Phillips said, " Try to tighten up the embouchure, Brick, as much as you can, and keep your mouthpiece warm."

They swung into a lively march as the students filed in. Paul took charge, and the program moved forward smoothly. Jeff kept trying to remember the first sentence of his speech, and found he hadn't the slightest idea what even the first word was.

Stage fright was a new experience to him. There seemed to be a gray cloud in his head. He did realize that Brick was keeping his horn to his mouth between numbers, when all instruments were supposed always to be at rest. But he remembered Mr. Phillips' admonition to keep the mouthpiece warm. He was irritated at being able to think of this, while his speech —

Across a long distance he heard Paul's voice. " One of the members of the band has a scheme he'd like to present to the student body. His name's Jeff Miles; here he is."

Jeff was in front of the microphone without knowing how he got there. A spattering of applause came up at him out of that sea of swimming faces. He cleared his throat and croaked. " Mr. Chairman."

And then from behind him a coarse " Blaa-at! " on a deep note of the baritone. Jeff looked over his shoulder in time to see Brick lowering his horn hastily, trying to look as if it had been an accident.

But Jeff knew, with sudden savage clarity, it had been no accident. Brick had been keeping his horn up all during the program for this moment. This, so to speak, was another blow in the fight that had taken place in the gym on an afternoon many weeks ago. One place Jeff had never lived was the Bronx, but he knew a Bronx cheer when he heard one.

The cloud in Jeff's mind evaporated abruptly in the heat of anger. He heard an uneasy titter go back along the rows.

" Maybe," he said, " I ought to sing, if there's going to be music."

The tension was drowned in a wave of laughter. More laughter, Jeff realized, than his remark justified. But he went on, then, to present his idea. His memory had not deserted him, after all.

As he turned from the microphone applause rolled up to him. Yet what he saw as he went toward his seat caused him to forget the applause.

Mr. Phillips was at the back of the band, leaning over a row of trombones. Even Jeff heard his undertone: *" Give me that horn! "* Brick turned and handed the director his instrument, red-faced and defiant.

That scene troubled Jeff all day. It nagged at the back of his mind even when, on two or three occasions, students stopped him in the hall to say, " Nice talk, Miles." He didn't want to be the cause of further trouble in the band.

Brick was not in his place that afternoon when rehearsal began. Jeff wanted mightily to ask Mel why, but felt somehow it was not the thing to do. The bell rang, the whistle blew, Rosie named the absentees and Mr. Phillips said: " You can take Brick's name off the roll. Permanently."

CHAPTER 7

T HAT EVENING Virginia said: " Jeepers! You went over in a big way at assembly this morning, and I know it was only because of my expert criticism beforehand. Betty Jean and I have our puppet show worked out, so now you have to listen to it before we give it next Wednesday on account of it's your turn to be tried out on."

" Wow! " said Jeff. " How you do get from here to there in a few well-chosen words! "

" How about us? " Dad grinned at the girl. "Don't you need any parental advice? "

" Certainly," said Ginny. " The bigger preview we have, the more it'll be like giving it to a real audience, and the better we'll do when we get in front of the class."

Mom spoke up. " Then let's include the Hardestys. I've been thinking, since they entertained us at Parkville, that we might have them over. If they could come to dinner Friday evening, you girls could give us your puppet play afterward."

" The whole family? " Jeff asked cunningly.

Ginny saw through him at once. " Meaning Carol too, Mom? "

" Of course," Mom laughed.

The Hardestys could come, a phone call revealed. Privately Jeff nurtured the hope that maybe this would develop into something, this neighboring back and forth. He made up his mind to be unusually nice to Ginny, for it was her doings that had started bringing the Hardestys and Mileses together.

He went off to school next morning in good spirits. Things were looking up, when you considered the whole picture. A little more than three months ago Jeff Miles had been a complete stranger here as he had been, on and off, in so many other schools. Now he was a member of the band, first chair in his section, and had even spoken to the student body on the band's behalf. Ahead was a concert on Thursday evening of next week, for which he felt reasonably well prepared. And, more immediately, he was anticipating an evening in company that would include the most attractive and outstanding girl in Garrison High. Not bad. Not bad at all.

Jeff put his horn in the band room, went to his locker, then climbed to the second floor to go to his American history class. His way took him past Senior Circle. The Circle was buzzing this morning, humming with excitement. Jeff wondered what was afoot.

" Miles! "

Jeff was startled. Paul Spencer beckoned to him. Puzzled, he made his way into the area not ordinarily open to underclassmen.

A sizable cluster of seniors were gathered around Paul, not an extraordinary circumstance, of course. There were Carol, Mel, Walt Terry, and others, all members of the band.

" Miles, how's about your asking Phillips to let Brick back into band? " Paul demanded.

For a moment Jeff could only stand and blink. The words he thought he'd heard simply didn't make sense. Finally he said cautiously, " Is this some sort of rib? "

" No," Paul snapped. " Since you were the one that got Brick kicked out of band, if you're willing to call it quits and tell Phillips so, he may listen."

Carol said: " Brick's really an awfully good egg, Jeff. He cuts up a lot and plays rough, I know, but honestly he doesn't mean half of it. The whole school saw what happened, and everybody will know why if he doesn't appear in the concert. He feels pretty terrible."

Jeff looked at her in astonishment. Was this the same girl who had been so friendly the other night?

" He'll cut seventh hour rather than go to study hall," Paul stated.

" I'm sure he'd do better if he got another chance," Mel said.

Walt added: " Seems like he got a kind of raw deal. Phillips was awfully tough on him."

" You've got next to Phillips, Miles," Paul summed it up. " You could square things if you wanted to."

Jeff debated. He didn't go for holding grudges, but what would he say to the director? That he didn't have to keep Brick out of band on his account? That certainly sounded egotistical.

He said slowly: " Phillips doesn't take to pressure. He's not letting anybody tell him how to run his band. I'd think it would be better for Brick to talk to him himself."

Carol said slowly: " Maybe Jeff has a point. Maybe it would seem to Mr. Phillips like butting in."

" That's the way it looks to me," Jeff answered. " I think it would do more harm than good."

" You mean you won't do it? " Paul demanded.

The tone caused Jeff to make up his mind. " No, I won't."

" We might have known! " answered Paul.

98

Jeff started to frame an answer, but it seemed pointless to argue. There was something phony about this deal, though at the moment he couldn't put his finger on it, exactly.

Not until later did it dawn on him how ridiculous it was for him to be put on the defensive. Corn's sake, Brick was the one in the wrong, yet Paul had twisted the whole thing around until — How fantastic could you get?

Evidently pretty fantastic, for the band that afternoon was upset again. Yesterday had been a sort of halfhearted rehearsal, but that could be charged to letdown after assembly. Today there was tempery, snappish resentment at being corrected, and as a result the playing was ragged, as if everybody nursed the feeling that Mr. Phillips was a harsh and ruthless taskmaster.

Thursday was not quite so bad. Friday Mr. Phillips laid down his baton wearily.

"I don't know," he remarked. "Maybe you'll snap out of it by next Thursday. I'd hate to be arrested for taking money for concert tickets under false pretenses."

Anyway the week was over. Jeff hurried home, anticipating the evening. Mom so arranged the dinner table that classmates should sit together, Betty Jean beside Ginny, and Carol beside Jeff. Dad lifted the silver cover from the roast.

"I had to stay at the store through lunch hour today," Mr. Hardesty said as Dad started carving. "At the looks of this dinner, I'm glad I did."

Mr. Miles began to serve the plates. "My work has taken this family to some odd dwellings in its time. Company houses, usually snagged halfway up a forty-degree mountain slope; rented apartments; log cabins. Once we lived in a house trailer at the foot of a mesa on a blazing desert. But, wherever, Ellen always manages to turn out a dinner that's an event."

"That," said Mrs. Hardesty, with the respect of one expert for another, "is a real achievement."

"You'll have me flustered in a minute," laughed Mrs. Miles.

The meal passed pleasantly. Later, in the living room, Ginny and Betty Jean set up their orange-crate theater and were ready to present their marionette show on Roman life and customs.

The scene, as announced by Betty Jean, was a street in front of the Roman senate late in the afternoon. As the curtains parted, two puppet men emerged from among quite realistic pillars. They moved jerkily on strands of number eight black thread, yet gave an impression of ponderous self-importance.

One man spoke in Virginia's best imitation of a pompous voice. "Well, Brutus Dumbus, it hath been a diem toughem in the senate."

A chuckle went through the audience.

"It hath indeed, Marcus Facilis," the other replied, in the deepest tones of Betty Jean. "Taxes! Taxes! Taxes! If we don't stop levying taxes, I shall lose my toga in the next plebiscite."

Both fathers responded to that with hearty laughter.

The two caricature politicians discussed the affairs of Rome awhile, and then Dumb Brute invited Easy Mark home to dinner. The second scene, at the home of Brutus Dumbus, gave the girls a chance to show Roman family life, and in the final scene the puppet people went to the circus, for which Betty Jean had created an impressive backdrop of the Colosseum. It was an altogether clever little play.

Everybody had warm praise for the girls' efforts and predicted a top grade for them on their report in Latin class.

Afterward the parents visited while Betty Jean and Ginny

packed up their show. They would take it to school on Wednesday. Jeff and Carol occupied themselves with the record player, which was in a corner of the dining room. It was a comfortable, friendly time and Jeff felt confidence building up in him. Perhaps he should ask what he had for some time been wanting to ask.

"The Drama Club play is a week from Wednesday evening, Carol. Would you go with me to see it?"

"Why, thank you, Jeff," Carol answered. "I'm sorry I already have a date for the play."

Jeff was disappointed, but in this matter he was determined. "I don't discourage easily," he grinned. "There's the Glee Club's Christmas program, basketball games coming up, and always the Garrison Theater."

Carol changed a record, her face thoughtful. "Jeff," she said, "some of the things that have happened must have given you an awfully poor impression of the Garrison kids. I've been trying to get it across to you that they're not really like that. I mean, I don't believe they've been exactly against you personally."

This was leading up, Jeff suspected, to a long refusal. He drawled, in the manner of his father, "Nothing that couldn't happen to any new kid, is that it?"

She flushed a bit. "No, that isn't quite it. If you were an ordinary person, it would be different. Everything is all tied up together, do you see?"

"No," Jeff admitted. "Let's start over. I asked you for a date."

"I think I should say no, and I'm really sorry."

"You and Paul are going steady?" he ventured, feeling he had nothing to lose.

"That means so many different things," the girl answered. "We have taken it for granted, I guess, that we would go together to the school social affairs this year. That isn't all of it, though."

"Then what is all of it?" he asked. "As far as I'm concerned, I can always depend on Paul to oppose anything I want to do."

"He doesn't like you because of what's happened to Mel and now to Brick," said Carol. "So if I have a date with you . . . Well, what has he ever done to me to deserve that?"

"He'd be sore at me, not you," Jeff surmised. "Sorer than he already is, if possible."

"Would that do you any good? But I'd be included too. For instance, we always went everywhere with Brick until the Parkville game, because Paul has no car. His father is dead and his mother works for the telephone company, and I guess they can't afford a car. Anyway, now he's stymied for transportation. So if I began dating you, and you have a car, how does that make me look — to him?"

"I didn't know that," said Jeff.

"You see what I mean about everything being all tied up together? It's even bad for the band for you and Paul to be against each other. Now if I took sides . . ."

Out of his disappointment Jeff said, "Haven't you?"

"I've tried not to," Carol returned steadily. She suddenly smiled. "Jeff, how would you like to make this corny? What about, for now, our just being good neighbors?"

Jeff forced himself to join her mood. "Hi, neighbor," he returned, and they shook hands.

The Mule Ear Mine was becoming for Jeff a reasonable facsimile of a hermit's cave, a retreat from a world that seemed at times to have more barriers than a half-mile hurdle course. He was glad when they got started for the mine the next day, glad to forget for a time that, despite their agreeable parting, Carol had chosen to retain Paul's company and reject his.

This day was the occasion for another family expedition. At long last Dad and Tony had got through the fault zone, and now could explore the workings on the other side. They were not extensive, but large enough, Dad assured Ginny, for her to find a place to label with a name she had thought up — "Gruesome Gulch."

The trip to the mine was difficult. Though winter had not yet come hard upon Garrison, it definitely had set in on Hoodoo Mountain. They drove with chains, through snow that increased in depth as they climbed to nearly a foot in some places along the road. Mountain country was at its best in winter, Mom declared. She wished again, as Jeff had heard her wish before, that tourists could more often see the vivid color of evergreens etched against the white sweep of snow slopes and the remote chill grandeur of lofty rock cliffs penciled by bold lines of crevices packed with ice. August, the height of the tourist season, was apt to be hot and dusty and dull by comparison.

The walk into the mountain along the mine track was a long one, these days. Almost exactly a fifth of a mile, Dad said. Ginny managed to walk beside Tony.

"There's going to be the swellest concert at school next Thursday," she told him. "Does Elfida like music?"

"Uh-oh!" Jeff said over his shoulder. "Watch it, Tony. You're getting a sales talk."

"You'd think it wasn't your old band I'm drumming up business for!" Ginny exclaimed. "Or your old Music Festival I'm helping raise money for. No fooling, Tony, the music's going to be supercilious — except maybe for the euphoniums. The tickets are only fifty cents, and —"

"I'll take two." Tony's laugh echoed along the tunnel.

"I remember the Garrison band is good, and I'm sure it has improved since Jeff has joined. Besides, Elfida *is* very fond of music."

They traversed the low, crowding passage through the fault zone, the heavy timbers of roof and walls seeming to bulge with the weight upon them. The tunnel on the other side felt generously roomy by contrast. It turned quite sharply to the left.

"Mean spot of track here," Dad observed. "That's a short curve, even for an ore car, and there's more grade coming down into the curve from beyond than I like. I guess the fact is I learned something about mining in the fifteen years since I drove this crosscut."

Jeff, in the lead, said, "Here's some new work."

"Sure thing. This is where we begin our two-hundred-and-ninety-three-foot search for the missing part of the Mule Ear."

"Or is it the Mule's other ear?" cracked Ginny.

"Ooh!" groaned Jeff.

"Anyway," Dad laughed, "you can see that the old tunnel turns right again here, along the vein I then thought was the Mule Ear extension." They walked on a few paces, as far as they could go.

Jeff scrutinized the irregular grayish streak that sloped down sharply from right to left across the face of the tunnel, moving his carbide lamp up and down along it. "Looks the same to me," he declared, "as what you can see of the Mule Ear on the other side."

"It does," Dad admitted, "but — I don't know. When you have lived with a vein as I did the Mule Ear, you get almost a feel for it. There are some small, but important, differences."

After a time Mom and Ginny returned to Garrison. Jeff,

with Dad helping him, set to work mucking out the shattered rock that had been dynamited loose the last thing yesterday afternoon. Tony worked above and ahead of them, drilling the next round of dynamite holes in the rock. The uproar of his drill seemed in itself enough to shake all the mountain loose. It was as if a whole collection of street repair crews had at one time decided to take up a section of paving.

As they worked, Jeff and Dad had to use care not to hit the air hose with pick or shovel. A line of iron pipe laid all the way in from the portal carried compressed air to the receiver. From this tank the air went to the drill, the last few feet by means of a flexible hose which could be pulled back out of harm's way during blasting.

When the ore car was full, Jeff prepared to take it out and dump it. Tony stopped his machine and climbed down.

" You drill awhile and I'll start loading the next car, Mr. Miles," he offered. " That shoveling gets strenuous."

" All right," agreed Dad. " What we need is two good men to muck while we drill and load the holes."

Jeff observed to Tony, as together they took the car down around the bad curve to start through the fault, " So you need lots more extra help? "

" You speed things up a lot," Tony told him, " but there's not enough of you. Your dad and I take turns and short-cut every way we can, but the drill is still shut off hours at a time. We could go at least a hundred per cent faster if we had two more men."

" You can't find two more men? "

" That's it," agreed Tony. He added, " You were the guy, though, that was worrying about your dad's capital holding out."

Jeff pondered the problem as he piloted the load. Every

day, until the mine produced, money was going out and none coming in. Eventually the family's savings would be gone, and each day of this slow progress brought that time so much nearer. With miners not to be had, this was more serious than the flooding had been, for it could go on indefinitely.

On the day of the band concert, December asserted itself in a driving snowstorm. So there'd be poor attendance! Maybe just as well, Jeff thought, the way rehearsals had continued. He went toward this last one, the dress rehearsal, feeling low.

As he passed through the lower hall, he came upon a strange scene. Paul was holding Brick's arm, and the two apparently were arguing heatedly.

"Heck with it!" Jeff heard Brick say. "They can't kick me out of school but once!"

Jeff couldn't make out Paul's reply, but it was urgent in tone.

"Nuts to the band concert!" Brick snapped. "I'm not hanging around to have any well-meaning characters say, 'Brick, we missed seeing you up there tonight.' And then saying behind my back they'd feared for a long time I'd come to a bad end! I'm blowing town for the night."

Jeff, moving on, heard no more. Paul arrived tardy at rehearsal, looking decidedly upset. Tardiness always irritated Mr. Phillips. The rehearsal got off to an uneven start. It did not improve.

When it was finally over, Carol said to Mr. Phillips, "They say a bad last rehearsal means a good performance."

Mr. Phillips shook his head. "I know they say that, but give me a good final rehearsal every time."

Evidently mountain folk like those of Garrison were not to be too much restricted by snow. When Jeff arrived at the building at seven fifteen, a few people were already coming in. The band gathered in their room for tuning and final instructions before going up to the stage.

" Where's Paul? " Mr. Phillips asked.

Heads turned around questioningly. Paul was not in the room, though the wall clock had moved past seven thirty. They mentioned the slippery streets and other possible causes of delay, and thought surely he'd be along any minute.

At a quarter of eight Paul came in. He went hurriedly for his horn, with no word to anybody except a brief, " Sorry," to Mr. Phillips. In his haste he dropped his mouthpiece. Something, Jeff was sure, was decidedly wrong.

There was no time for further thought. They proceeded upstairs and arranged themselves on stage. At exactly eight o'clock the curtains swept open.

The room was well filled, and when Mr. Phillips came out to mount the podium, generous applause greeted him. He bowed and stepped up, but before he raised the stick he spoke in an undertone that could not be heard by the audience.

" This tells the tale, kids . . . whether we get these people's support for our festival or not. If you've got what it takes, let's have it now."

Jeff hit the first note of " The Thunderer " sharp, clean, and high. No time to be thinking they'd played this a million times before and he'd never liked the piece very well. What was needed now was enthusiasm. He held in to give the reeds their chance on the first strain. It was going better than rehearsal, certainly.

They were into the trio, the trumpets bugling nicely, when Jeff thought suddenly one of the clarinets had gone wild. No, it was a siren! Outside. Far off. A disconcerting sound, but in a moment they hit the breakup strain, and the outside noise was drowned out.

"Whack! Whack! Whack! Whack!"

Mr. Phillips struck the stand for two measures and called urgently: "Basses! You're lagging!"

They got through the piece and the audience applauded, but they'd have to do better. The next number was a concert overture and, to Jeff's immense relief, they did do better. In fact, they seemed to have worked off their shakiness in that first march, and the music became smoother as the concert proceeded.

Except for the basses. Usually the four sousaphones furnished a dependable, substantial foundation, but tonight that was lacking. Once or twice Jeff listened for that deep, solid "Pom-pom" to open a phrase. He heard it only faintly and uncertainly. The disturbance in Paul was being reflected in the whole section.

The last number was "The Stars and Stripes Forever," and as the various sections stood to state their versions of the famous trio, the lift and swing of it spread. With the final strain, the whole band standing, horns shouting, fifes shrilling, cymbals crashing, every member was caught up in the majestic chorus on a wave of unity. It was like that moment in the Lamont game, only this was even more magnetic in its togetherness.

A storm of applause burst over them at the finish. They remained standing a few seconds, then sat down, then rose again at a gesture from Mr. Phillips to receive the crowd's tribute. The director's face was shining. The curtain was closed, and had to be opened again before the audience was satisfied.

When the band was dismissed, instead of going home the players gathered in the band room to talk excitedly, to relive that magic interval when everything had been, it seemed, absolutely perfect.

Everyone was pleased, not only with the performance as a whole, but with himself. Mr. Phillips had never been funnier. The only person not sharing in this was Paul. Paul, Jeff noticed when he looked around, was missing. Either he had not come to the band room or he had left immediately. That seemed odd.

They were finally casing up and preparing to leave, some at the urging of parents who had come down to take youngsters home, when Paul re-entered the room. His band cap and overcoat were powdered with snow.

"Where you been, Spencer?" Walt Terry shouted jovially.

"Down at the corner drug to phone the hospital," Paul replied, and something in his tone jarred the room to silence. "Brick went off the road this evening."

Mr. Phillips repeated, unbelievingly, "Brick went off the road?"

Paul nodded, misery giving ghastliness to his white face. "He couldn't take it, being here and not being in the concert. He started driving over to Parkville. Up on Bedroll Pass he hooked bumpers with a pickup truck and turned over three times. That siren we heard during the first number was the ambulance bringing him in."

After a hush Mel asked, "How do you know that?"

"My mother was to get off work at the phone office at seven o'clock. I went by to bring her to the concert. The emergency calls were just coming in. That's why I was late."

Jeff thought, *And he played the whole concert knowing that!* Aloud he said, "How bad is he?"

"They don't know at the hospital," said Paul, "whether he'll live or die."

109

CHAPTER 8

THE ATMOSPHERE of the halls was strangely heavy the next week of school, little knots of sober students exchanging in subdued voices bits of information about the accident.

There was no other topic of conversation. Before, to practically all of them, traffic tragedies had been something reported in the newspaper. Something that had happened away off some place, for car wrecks were rare in the Garrison area. Mountain highways, despite their appearance, are safer than most; their curves and grades and heights tend to inspire caution.

" They say his leg was broken in three places."

" Fractured collarbone and lacerations too, I heard."

" Shock's the most dangerous part. If they can pull him through the shock . . ."

" Are you over eighteen? You can donate blood for transfusions if you're eighteen."

" I heard he had a lot of transfusions. I forget how many."

" In surgery three hours and a half."

" What about the pickup truck? Who was in it? "

" Man and wife and little girl. Little girl had a broken arm, but that was all. Truck was messed up, of course."

" Thanks be, he didn't kill somebody! "

" The State Patrol says he must have been going at least

sixty."

Talk like that, kept up endlessly, cast a pall over the whole school. Little was accomplished in any class, including band. The end of the week marked the beginning of Christmas vacation. This was fortunate, for the school as a whole needed a change of concern. The word Friday afternoon was that the doctors thought Brick, barring complications, would live, quite probably not be crippled.

Jeff was relieved. It had been hard to endure the constant thought of Brick lying up there at the hospital. Because Brick had not been a friend, he found himself with a tendency, vague but painful, to tell himself that he should have treated Brick better. The only way to shake this discomfort was to ask himself how he could have acted differently. He found inner debate an unsteadying thing.

The Mule Ear Mine was what he needed. Good old ornery granite that resisted his pick and exhausted his back and kept his mind on primary matters like bracing his shoulders or getting his feet out of the way of tumbling chunks. That first Saturday morning of vacation, he entered enthusiastically upon a two weeks' period when he could be a regular member of the Mule Ear's crew.

For now the Mule Ear had a crew, loosely speaking. Dad had finally been able to hire one miner, which was a beginning, of sorts.

"Name's Farnum," he introduced himself to Jeff with a horn-palmed handshake. "Winfield Stratton Farnum. Yes, sir. Named for a famous miner. Been in minin' all my life."

"I'm glad to know you, Mr. Farnum," said Jeff.

The miner spat tobacco juice through whiskers of a color undecided between white and brown. "Folks call me Windy," he stated. "Yes, sir. Short for my first name. You too, Bub. Feel more at home without any misterin'.""

From then on Farnum was Windy and Jeff was Bub. Windy had had, it appeared, a vast experience with mines.

" Yes, sir. Worked in some real mines in my day. Don't find such operations any more. You take the old Central. There was a tunnel. Nine thousand feet. Mules for haulage, with cars in trains and every car carryin' better'n a yard o' rock."

" Would you like to change sides? " Jeff offered. " Shoveling left-handed doesn't bother me."

He and Windy had the job of mucking out, while Dad and Tony drilled and loaded the holes. Jeff saw that he was doing about two thirds of the shoveling while most of Windy's energy went to keeping the conversation interesting.

With a car loaded, Jeff helped Windy get it over the bad spot in the track.

" Yes, sir," Windy observed, " none o' this baby buggyin' in the big mines. You take the Siwatch. Solid mile o' works, and electric locomotives pullin' the cars. That makes 'er safe."

When Jeff and his father arrived home that evening, Dad said: " Don't anybody talk to Jeff. His ear's bent way down onto his shirt collar already."

Jeff returned the grin.

Dad chuckled. " If we could get all of Windy's hot air in the pipe, we wouldn't need the compressor. But I believe the old fellow does know mining, and maybe he'll do more as he gets toughened to the work."

" I'm surprised he'd work for such a small operator as you," teased Jeff.

" You know what? It's only because I'm a graduate engineer with — I quote — ' a mighty fine reppy-tation.' So help me!"

Windy continued to be amusing, and he did become more productive. Yet always his tongue went faster than his shovel, and his tales were interesting and flavorful. He began to exhibit a slam-bang way of handling tools and ore cars that sometimes roused uneasiness in Jeff.

"Aw, swing loose, Bub," Windy would say. "You ain't gonna knock down this mountain with a stray bump."

When vacation was over, Jeff found school more normal. Brick was reported at home now, making a steady recovery. Band rehearsals within two or three days once more followed the pattern of regular routine. Jeff returned to diligent, systematic practice.

Then one evening toward the middle of the second week of school, while the Miles family was at dinner, the phone rang.

Ginny said, "I'll get it." Then she called: "Dad, it's for you. Tony Vasquez."

"Tony!" exclaimed Dad. "Where's he calling from?"

"I don't know," the girl answered, "but he sounded urgent."

Dad's voice, too, soon took on an urgent sound. Jeff, Ginny, and their mother sat, their dinner forgotten, until he strode quickly back into the room.

"Is something wrong, John?" Mrs. Miles asked.

"Yes," Dad admitted. "Accident at the mine. Rockfall. Tony brought a car through the timbered section and was going back to help Windy with another. Heard a great racket. When he got there, the tunnel was sealed off."

"Windy!" Mom gasped. "Is he —?"

"Windy didn't get out." Dad went for his wraps, moving fast. "That's all Tony knows. Anything else is guesswork."

"I'll be right with you." Jeff took the stairs two at a

time. When he returned in boots and sheepskin, he found Mom pouring coffee into a thermos and Ginny bringing heavy ear muffs.

"Should we call the police or the fire department?" the girl asked.

"No. They couldn't extend their services to the mines. We'll have a look first. The cave-in may not be too far through. If we can't handle it, I'll send out a call for volunteer help. Come down as far as Owlet Lodge and phone in, as Tony did. Mr. Hardesty would lend a hand, I know, and there would be other townspeople."

"I'll stay close by the phone," Mom promised.

The drive up Hoodoo Gulch was painfully slow. Jeff, his senses sharp with tension, took the icy stretches almost by feel, edging the truck in the direction of the skid on some of the banked curves, using always as high a gear as the grade permitted despite his overpowering urge to shift into low-low and tromp on the accelerator.

"If the car got loose and ran ahead of Windy, he's all right." Dad broke the silence finally. "The stuff would have come down before he was close enough to be caught."

"Suffering mainly for want of someone to talk to," Jeff guessed. It helped to speak of it matter-of-factly. Kept back the chill of picturing Windy lying pinned under tons — That was no good. Panic was the worst possible thing.

There was the usual filling of carbide lamps at the mine portal. It took a maddeningly long time. But feverish haste was the next worst thing to panic. When finally they got going, they began, two thirds of the way in, to hear a faint chock! chock! Tony swinging a pick!

"Am I glad you're here!" Tony shouted when they reached him. He was hacking at a tumble of rocks and dirt and timbers wedged solidly from the tunnel roof to the floor. " I didn't want to stop hammering at the thing. If Windy can hear . . . I don't want him to think we're letting up."

Dad stepped in Tony's place and took up the pick. " Jeff, you shovel back for me. Tony, catch your breath and then throw the stuff farther back. We'll take turns. If we can go easy, so we don't keep knocking more down all the time . . ."

Jeff found a curious sense of unreality about it all. Scoop, lift, throw! A thin pile of debris rising steadily along the tunnel wall. Shift to Dad's position. Then to Tony's. A corner of the overturned ore car began to be in the way.

" Must have been coming with terrific speed," Jeff guessed.

" No," said Dad. " Didn't have far enough to get up momentum. Just enough to leave the track and careen along the timbers."

Tony said: " If it knocked out one timber, the weight of the rock would do the rest. Hand me the crowbar, will you? "

Doggedly they slogged on. Jeff lost track of how many times they shifted, how many timbers they wrestled loose. The night wore on. Not that day outside would make any difference here. He pried and rolled out a hundred-pound chunk of rock.

" Hey! "

They stared at the barrier, at one another, not daring to believe that the faint sound was more than a scraping of rock on rock.

" Windy! " Dad roared. " Windy! Are you O.K.? "

Some loose pebbles slithered down. On the end of the small sound rode a distant, " Ay-ee-ee."

Jeff looked at his watch. It was 3:33. They bowed their

backs in savage concentration.

At a few minutes past four Windy's voice said clearly: " I see your light. I'll start mine. Put 'er out to save air."

A faint gleam appeared in a crevice of the mass.

" We'll have you out in no time." Dad spoke reassuringly. " Jeff, the coffee."

Jeff ran all the way to the truck for the thermos Mom had filled.

By five they had scraped a hole close to the ore car, which braced back the weight above, and Windy inched through, grumbling something about " a dad-gummed water snake." When they could reach his hands, they pulled him free.

" Thank heaven! " Dad said feelingly.

" Dad-gummed sprag musta broke," Windy began, his talkativeness restored abruptly with his safety. " I was walkin' up the track. Tony was gonna come help me get the car down the grade. First thing I knowed, I seen the car comin' at me like the Pony Express. I seen I couldn't stop 'er. I dove to the inside of the curve. Grabbed 'er as she went past, but she tore outa m' grip. If I'd ahad time to get my balance, I mighta steadied 'er up and got 'er through, but I never."

Jeff saw Dad and Tony exchange glances. He understood. Even he didn't believe the story.

Dad said, " If you'd waited for Tony . . ."

" Wa'n't nothin' Tony coulda did that I didn't do. No, sir, John, that's just a plumb dangerous layout. Too dangerous for me. I'm drawin' my time! "

" You — " Dad began, and then stopped. You could almost see him counting mentally to ten. But all he said aloud was, " I'll write you a check when we get to Tony's cabin."

He and Tony and Jeff were in worse shape than Windy. The long, tense night had left all three of them at the stumbling point, exhausted.

116

Garrison was just stirring to begin a new day's business when Jeff headed the truck up Main Street, Dad and Windy beside him. They stopped in front of a business block that had a fourth-rate hotel on the second floor. Windy got out and lifted his battered cheap brown suitcase.

"Windy." Dad's tone made Jeff jump. "You had orders that one man was never to take a car down that grade by himself. Breaking my orders, you came close to getting yourself killed and left us with a good many days' unnecessary work rebuilding that section of tunnel. Now you're walking out, leaving me shorthanded. Don't go spreading a story that the Mule Ear's a dangerous mine and make it harder for me to get a crew. Understand?"

Windy said solemnly, "Mr. Miles, my lips is sealed."

As they drove on, Dad shook his head.

"Wow!" said Jeff. "Did you ever pin his ears back!"

"It did no good," Mr. Miles answered, "except to get a load off my chest. Poor old codger. He could no more keep his mouth shut than I could stop breathing. Which is why he's living — existing — in this dreary, hopeless way. That, and his poor work. He's never done a good job at anything, so he has to talk a big job. Well, we can't take care of Windy. I don't even see how we're going to take care of ourselves, with the setback this cave-in has given us."

"Let me take a few days from school," Jeff suggested, "and help get the thing cleaned up."

"We're not that ruined," Dad said. "I guess I'm tired. Excuse me."

"No, but honest. My grades are in good shape. I could send word to my teachers by Ginny. And this is an emergency."

"It's an emergency, all right," Dad admitted.

So the arrangement was finally made. Jeff spent five days

in the Mule Ear, struggling with caving rock and splintered timbers. By the end of those days they had restored the tunnel through the fault and Dad and Tony were ready once more to take up their slow grind back in the crosscut.

Two men to do the work of four or five!

Jeff had a fresh appreciation for school that Wednesday, regardless of the amount of make-up work he had accumulated. He was ready, but definitely, to emphasize mind rather than muscle for a while.

Mr. Phillips said, "Take ' Poet and Peasant. ' " And added, " I expect this will be one of the required festival numbers." The music proved to be a stimulating new adventure for Jeff. Indeed, the whole rehearsal made him realize how much he had missed the day-by-day pleasure of band.

Next morning he went to school early to check some make-up assignments with his teacher of solid geometry. When he came out of the math room, he stopped short. Entering at the far end of the hall was a familiar redheaded figure.

More exactly, only part of the head was now red. One side was plastered with adhesive tape. There was a sling, and a cumbersome white cast, and a crutch. Alongside, a tall blond-haired figure moved solicitously. Almost at once kids began to converge on the two, more and more, Jeff thought, as though the Pied Piper of Hamelin had been playing his young people's music.

Brick Lassiter had returned to school!

Jeff heard countless hearty greetings: " Hi, Brick, old boy! "

" It's good to see you, guy! "

" Hey, can you shoot pool with that stick? "

Brick's going up the stairs was a slow, triumphal procession. The throng waited in the hall outside the office while

Brick went in to get his absence excuse. When he came back out, they swept him up again, so that Jeff was reminded of a team hoisting their star to their shoulders. Brick, though the freckles stood out almost harshly against his pallor, wore a huge grin. The crowd ushered him into Senior Circle, where he leaned against a window sill, and one by one the receiving line moved forward to write their names on the plaster of his leg cast.

Almost six hours later, as the band gathered, excitement was still high.

"Did you see Brick?"

From one of the girls: "Kid, isn't he pathetic? To think, if he hadn't been kicked out of band . . ."

"I could have just bawled! The poor guy!"

Paul arrived late and out of breath. "I had to help Brick out to his car — his dad's car," he explained.

The band played uncertainly. Full-volume passages were rough, and softer passages too loud. Once Jeff saw Sylvia Dodd brush at her face as if wiping away tears. Everybody seemed keyed up, terrifically.

Next day was no better. They were playing as raggedly, Jeff thought, as they had been before the concert last month. They were doing "Poet and Peasant," or trying to, when Mr. Phillips stopped them.

"Bill," he said, "one alto sax just doesn't bring out that solo strong enough without pushing. Isn't the passage cued into the baritone part, Jeff?"

Jeff nodded.

"Then you take it too," directed Mr. Phillips, "to help Bill out. Some arrangements have it as a baritone solo anyway."

"Then give it to Jeff," said Bill Hayes, and there was an edge to his voice.

Jeff felt as surprised as Mr. Phillips looked. Then embarrassed, and then angry. What on earth was biting Bill?

"Now," drawled Mr. Phillips, "leave us not be tetchy. We're simply growing two solos where only one grew before."

Jeff had no choice but to go ahead and play the notes in small print, but it was not good. Whether he was off, or whether the band simply messed up the accompaniment, he could not tell. But after two unsatisfactory efforts, they left the solo and went on through the rest of the piece. Struggled through, rather, for certainly it was about as rough as anything they'd ever done.

After rehearsal Jeff made his way across the room. Bill Hayes was casing his horn. He looked up at Jeff and rose.

"Sorry I opened my big mouth, Miles." He spoke fast and walked away rapidly.

On his way home Jeff looked back to see Paul and Carol coming slowly down the hill toward her house. Jeff waited in his living room until he saw Paul go on, then went outside and up to the corner. Carol opened to his ring.

"Hello, neighbor," Jeff grinned. "You're the most efficient interpreter I know. How's about a quick translation?"

"You don't make sense," smiled the girl, "but come in."

As he stepped inside, Jeff explained: "I'd like to know what was the matter with Bill Hayes today. You've helped me before in understanding the score around here. Would you again?"

Carol hesitated. "I don't know," she said then, "but my guess is he was upset and on edge, the way a lot of people are. You see, those of us who have known Brick all our lives, and remember him as so happy-go-lucky and everything — well, it does something to us to see him the way he is now."

"I can imagine it would."

"Then there are some I-told-you-so's around. I suppose there always are."

"I-told-you-so's?"

"Kids that say Brick was bound to crash sooner or later, the way he drove. As if they'd never taken chances in their own driving and happened to be lucky. That kind of person can make you so mad!"

Jeff nodded, but refrained from comment. This wrangle among the people who had grown up together was one in which he was not involved. He said only, "I'm glad it wasn't something I'd done that burned Bill."

"There are lots of sore tempers since this came up. It's in the air."

"That's bad," said Jeff soberly. "Well, thanks for interpreting." He took his leave.

Another week dragged by. The band seemed unable to accomplish anything.

Mr. Phillips continued patient. "You're a count behind, clarinets. Let's try it again."

A muttered undertone would be heard: "If Jim'd play his part so you could hear . . ."

Next thing the first trombone wasn't speaking to the third French horn. One snare drummer and one trumpeter were passing each other with stony stares. Could all this, Jeff wondered, be coming out of that pointless argument Carol had mentioned? Brick's accident was history, and a court hearing had been held to determine responsibility. Jeff had heard that Brick's driving license had been taken up for a year. Didn't that settle it?

Oddly, Jeff now seemed to be making unusual progress at getting acquainted. Players in the flute section and the reed section and the percussion section, fifteen or twenty students who had never before paid any particular attention to him, started going out of their way, it almost appeared, to pass greetings with him. It was becoming a habit, as they settled in places for warm-up, to send a wave and a grin across the room.

Jeff did some wondering. By some queer quirk were they turning to him because they had fallen out with certain of their long-time associates? Jeff had no way of knowing. Contrasted with the easy, comradely spirit of the organization when he had first known it, this was appalling.

Often during this interval Jeff recalled those terse words of Mr. Phillips: " The one thing a band has to be is together." This one wasn't any longer, and seemed to be drifting farther apart. You could, as Carol had said, feel hurt and anger in the air.

When they had endured through to the end of the seventh hour on Friday, Mr. Phillips said: " You're dismissed, except for Paul and Carol and Henrietta and Jeff. I want to see those four."

Jeff saw Paul and Carol look at each other inquiringly. " Have we done something? " he asked Henrietta Ralston, the tall, shy librarian.

" I was about to ask you the same thing," the girl answered.

" Take a load off your feet," called Mr. Phillips when everyone else had gone. They sat in a row and he regarded them across his desk. None of them was misled by his droll manner into thinking this wasn't business. He drawled: " This band is going to pot. Correction. It has gone to pot."

The blunt statement, though they knew its truth, jarred them.

After a moment Paul said, " You see, maestro, it's like this . . ."

Mr. Phillips took it up promptly. " Some think one way

and the rest think the opposite. Hard feelings. I know that. How much does that pay on any quiz show?"

Whatever Paul had in mind to say, that stopped him. Jeff was wondering why he himself was included in this. The row had passed him by. Henrietta too, so far as he knew.

"This was to be Garrison High's big year," Mr. Phillips resumed. "Would have been the year by which we'd measure all other years, except for the band. Band had a chance to host the regional music festival, but the organization went all to flinders. So we say this year the band is rebuilding. That's a football nicety meaning the present outfit is a flop." His caustic remarks seemed directed at Paul.

The head boy flushed red. "What's wrong is something I can't do anything about," he declared.

"I believe you could," Mr. Phillips countered. "I directed a church choir once, a gossipy, disorganized group that sang like a bunch of cats fighting. Along in November that year I managed to get a quartet started, a strong leading voice in each part. Those four began working together, singing together, until it was like one of those dreams out of a Wagner opera. They brought that choir along until at Easter, when they sang the 'Hallelujah Chorus,' there wasn't a dry eye in the house."

He stopped, evidently waiting.

At last Carol ventured, "I guess we don't quite know what you're leading up to, Mr. Phillips."

"I notice," said Henrietta, "that there are four of us."

"Go to the head of the class," said Mr. Phillips. "Soprano, alto, tenor, and bass." He stabbed a finger at Carol, Henrietta, Jeff, and Paul in turn.

Now Jeff understood why they were here, but — corn's sake! "You mean the four of us work together the way you described?"

"Now you're at the head of the class. The most competent player in each of your parts. If this band can be pulled together, it'll be through your leadership."

From Paul came a stifled, "Oh, no!"

"Meaning?" Mr. Phillips asked sharply.

"We — I — I work Tuesday, Thursday, and Saturday evenings. I belong to a lot of other organizations . . . all the extra things as head boy. I just wouldn't have the time to give it." Paul was, Jeff thought, desperately dragging up excuses.

Jeff also was floored by the idea. He and Paul had tangled from the first, and every time they spoke it got worse. For the two of them to try to work closely —

"You have time for a lot of other organizations and extras." Mr. Phillips spoke very quietly. "Like everybody else, you have time to do those things you want to do. If you don't want to do this, you might as well say so straight out."

Anger shook Paul. "All right, I don't!"

"Why?" Mr. Phillips was being merciless.

"We couldn't work together!"

"You and Jeff couldn't work together. Is that it? Isn't that exactly what's broken up this band?"

"Why," said Jeff, since the director seemed to be looking at him, "no. I thought it was something about Brick Lassiter."

"And why did this happen to Brick?" Paul challenged.

Jeff leaped to his feet, but Mr. Phillips was already speaking. He sank down again.

"Many reasons," said the director. "For one, I dismissed him from band not, as some people say, because of Jeff, but because he never took his bandsmanship seriously and his horseplay became a nuisance. For another, though I'd rather not say it, he showed poor judgment of driving conditions."

"There's plenty," Paul cried bitterly, "ready to kick him when he's down! Crippled up, his car wrecked, even his driver's license gone!"

"If you want to help him get on his feet," Mr. Phillips said, "that's fine. While you're at it, help him get wise to himself. But stop using him to play on people's decent sympathies. It isn't necessary to blame somebody and create factions and split this band apart. I'm not ordering you to like each other. If band means enough to you, if the success of this school year means enough to you —" Mr. Phillips shifted in his chair. "How about you, Henrietta? Will you work in this quartet?"

Henrietta gave a start. "Why, yes, I like the idea. It might be fun."

"Carol?"

"Certainly." Carol managed a smile. "It could still be fun. Now that we've let our hair down completely, can't we forget all this?"

No, Jeff thought, as Mr. Phillips looked at him, we can't simply forget it. But if, as Mr. Phillips said, the success of the band depended on it — nobody knew how much the band meant to him.

"I'll work at it," he said.

"Your decision, Paul," Mr. Phillips summed it up.

"Decision!" Paul grated. "What can I say, after the way you've all framed it onto me?"

"I don't know." The director suddenly grinned. "What can you say?"

Paul looked uncertain. "Why, I'll have to go along, of course. Are you satisfied?"

"For the time being, yes." Mr. Phillips rose briskly. "First I want you to work out every number in the band's repertory so you can lead out. Then here are parts for you — the quartet music from *Rigoletto*. Get that learned so perfectly that the harmony melts in your mouths. When will you have your first rehearsal?"

Carol offered, "Tomorrow afternoon at my house?"

"We're supposed to go to Brick's tomorrow afternoon," Paul told her.

"Oh, yes. And you work tomorrow evening."

"Sunday afternoon, then," suggested Henrietta. "My folks and I can stay in town after church and I'll come to Carol's house."

A jumble of thoughts raced through Jeff's head as he made his way home. He was sick at Paul's vicious accusation that he was responsible for what had happened to Brick.

Plainly Paul hated him — there was no point to asking why. And yet they'd just now agreed to work together!

It would be a nice trick if they could do it, he thought. Anyway, whether they could or not, there was nothing for it but to try.

CHAPTER 9

An AGREEMENT was an agreement, Jeff realized, and this one sounded very good in principle . . . until he started wondering exactly how he'd spend an afternoon at the Hardestys' in the company of Paul Spencer.

As he went through his duties at the Mule Ear next day, the actualities didn't look so good. Would he and Paul speak? What would they say? do? He couldn't just ignore the guy's existence, not in the same room doing the same thing, and Paul couldn't ignore his. They couldn't decently keep the air hostile and make the girls uncomfortable. It was no use kidding himself he could pretend everything was hunky-dory, either.

Jeff decided, as he pushed a loaded ore car out through the tunnel, to wait and see what Paul did — and keep his guard up. If Paul wanted to be civil, O.K. If he wanted to be frosty, O.K. too. With temperatures what they were at the Mule Ear the last of January, Jeff was prepared to play a game of freeze-out with a snowbank if necessary.

He lost no time getting back into the comparative mildness of the mine. It looked very much a going concern now, the well-kept track leading through the shipshape windings of the tunnel. The air pipe above the drainage ditch, the neat stacks of supplies in the safety bays at the side, the solidly protective bulk of the timbers lining the course through the fault — all these gave the whole workings a stout appearance.

Beyond the fault Jeff switched his empty car to a stub track built back a little way into the old workings. He spragged the wheels and left it, and walked on into the new tunnel that turned aside at the switch.

As the lamps of his father and Tony came in sight, the tunnel became less neat. Chunks of rock had been rolled to one side of the track, protruding corners of granite stuck out of walls and ceilings, the floor was littered, and the ties and rails were strung along on top of it, unevenly.

"You take a few minutes' rest while Tony and I finish loading, Jeff," Dad ordered. "Then I'll take the car out, you can start filling an empty, and Tony can drill another hole, or maybe two."

"It goes un-fast, doesn't it?" Jeff asked as he sat down.

Dad and Tony had another car three fourths loaded, but three or four more carloads would have to be moved before they could begin drilling again. Then there would be six or eight more holes to drive — they fired fourteen charges at a blasting — and then a wait until smoke and dust had cleared so that the air would be fit to breathe again, and finally the slow, laborious process of mucking out.

"We're forty-two inches farther along than we were when you were here last Saturday," Tony said. "That's better than eight inches a day on the average."

"How much farther do you figure we have to go, Dad?" asked Jeff.

"I'd say about two hundred feet."

Jeff did some quick mental arithmetic. "Corn's sake! That'll take a year at this rate!"

Dad nodded. "We'll have to get some kind of crew before

long, and I think we will. Every time we blast and have to wait for the air to clear, I go to town and hunt men. With two good men we could make a foot and a half a day, or better, and start thinking about four or five months. But I may have to settle for anybody I can get."

Jeff gave the problem some sober study as the day went on. He didn't know — probably Dad didn't know — exactly how long the Miles family could continue to live and operate a mine without an income. Last fall Mom had showed concern at the prospects of a year. That would be till September. Jeff guessed that probably they were O.K. until school was out.

By June the Mule Ear would have to be paying. If it didn't, Jeff didn't know what Dad could do but get another job with a large mining company. That would take him to — name practically any state, or even another country. Soon the family would follow. They didn't like having Dad away from home. Sell 645 Spruce Street and the Mule Ear, if anybody would buy. At least the equipment. Then go on the move again.

What Jeff would have had out of this venture was one whole year in the same school, a chance to find out whether permanence made the difference he'd always thought it did. That whole year was half gone, and so far he didn't have much to show for his permanence. His findings were about as much barren granite as the stuff Dad was blasting out of the tunnel.

When Sunday afternoon finally arrived, Jeff packed up his horn, music stand, and band folio and walked up to the Hardestys'. Henrietta was already there. Jeff sat down beside her and began unfolding his stand. The doorbell rang, Carol went to answer it, and Paul entered.

He came in flashing his nod, wink, and grin. "Hiya,

folks!" Since only Henrietta and he were in the room, Jeff thought this must include him.

Jeff said, "Hi," as Henrietta said, "Hello."

They talked over which piece they should start on, the discussion going impersonally from one to another. They chose a march. Then came the question of how they could get started together.

"Suppose I tap it out with my foot for what would be two measures," Paul suggested, "and we all come in on the next 'One.'"

Corn's sake, this wasn't going to be so bad, after all! For once, all the parts flowed out with no stumblings or sour notes. The music sounded different, better than it ever had before.

They moved on to some of the more difficult numbers. On these they had to stop at times and work out a passage. Still it was a pleasure, playing with musicians as competent as these when they were playing competently. By remembering to speak with careful politeness to Paul, Jeff saw that he was going to be able to avoid any unpleasantness. Forming this quartet was a pretty sharp idea! A gold medal for Mr. Phillips.

On one number they ran into a snag. No matter how carefully they worked the passage, it didn't sound right. They tried it once more.

"No, no, honey. You're hitting it on the beat. It's after-time."

Astonished, Jeff looked around to see Mr. Hardesty coming in from the next room, laying down his newspaper as he came. "Here." He reached for Carol's horn.

Wiping the mouthpiece with a handkerchief, he put the instrument to his lips and ran up and down its register, the full two octaves, rapidly, with that rattling effect a trumpeter gives when doing scales. Jeff sat openmouthed.

Then Mr. Hardesty said, "Let's take it again."

They touched their notes, and Jeff fairly jumped out of his shoes. Mr. Hardesty hit those troublesome tones in brilliant, brazen, lifting calls that turned the knotty passage into a blaze of glory.

"I get it," said Carol, as her father returned the trumpet.

"Corn's sake!" Jeff breathed.

"Oh, you don't know about my past," laughed Mr. Hardesty. "I was first trumpet with a traveling orchestra once upon a time. We played Garrison, and a certain lady here so took my fancy that — well, here I am a hardware merchant."

"I knew you were chairman of the Chamber of Commerce music committee," said Jeff.

"I enjoy having some connection with a band. I don't know anything where everybody in it has a part, so literally. I hope you kids are enjoying every minute of it. Nothing else will ever give you as good a chance to really get together. In a band you can feel it. You hear when you're together."

"Or when you're not," returned Carol.

"That's just the working phase. You know what I mean. Ever see a barbershop quartet, how they le-an into a piece?" Mr. Hardesty drew the word out graphically. "That's the way you four ought to get."

Henrietta asked, "Couldn't you stay around, Mr. Hardesty, and help us out in the hard spots?"

He did, and they played on.

But Jeff played absent-mindedly for a time. *Probably* Mr. Hardesty had put into words what he had been feeling toward for a long time, ever since that magical moment in the Lamont game. And again since the concert, during

their playing of "The Stars and Stripes Forever." Togetherness!

That was what it was about a band. At moments like
those you belonged. It was a part of you and you were a
part of it, and there was nothing else like it anywhere that
Jeff knew of.

That was what had kept him in band, Jeff knew now, in
spite of Paul's sniping and all the difficulties and annoy-
ances and hard, tedious work. It would continue to keep
him there, because in all his life — moving often, a
stranger often, lonely often — those moments of togetherness were the ones when he felt he really belonged. And
that was the feeling he wanted most.

Before he knew it, it was dark, and Mrs. Hardesty announced to the quartet that she had fixed them a chili supper. After they were seated in the dark-paneled Hardesty
dining room, Carol said, "Maybe we ought to plan when
and where we're going to have more rehearsals."

"You're welcome to come here any time," said Mrs.
Hardesty.

"Evenings aren't so good for me," Henrietta said with
some apology. "It's quite a trip in, and Dad and Mother
don't like me to make it alone at night. They could come
with me sometimes."

"Do I understand you live on a ranch?" asked Jeff.

"Yes, Turkey Track Ranch. Fifteen miles out. The Ralston ancestors took it up practically in the wake of Zebulon
Pike, I guess."

"And you drive to and from school every day?"

"Does she!" Carol answered. "Not only that, she has a
straight A average."

"Highest in the senior class," added Paul, "and the
youngest too, aren't you, Henrietta?"

The girl nodded and looked a little self-conscious.

"Boy," Jeff grinned, "am I ever out of place around such an intellect!"

"A good thing you didn't say 'brain,'" Henrietta returned. "I've seriously considered flunking so that I could have a good time for a year."

"That's what Brick did, sort of," Paul remarked, and the conversation fell off suddenly.

"We still haven't worked out any rehearsal plans," Carol stated presently. "Let's try to stay away from evenings, so as not to inconvenience Henrietta."

"I'm tied up certain afternoons," Paul said, speaking with care, "on Spencer's Swingsters."

"On what?" asked Jeff.

"Spencer's Swingsters. I'm working up a dance band. Eight of us. Fellows that are close friends and really enjoy playing together."

Jeff caught his meaning. The quartet members were not close friends and did not enjoy working together. So the uneasy truce of cold politeness was ended and an ambush warfare of sniping insults declared.

Mr. Hardesty said: "You have the type of personality to make a good dance band director, Paul. I expect you'll like it."

"I do," Paul nodded. "It's recreation as well as work. We meet up at Brick's place, in his rumpus room. It helps him pass the time while he's shut in. We can take our dates along and have a listening audience to give us comments and suggestions. When we get tired rehearsing, we give Brick a lift with his make-up work, have refreshments. It's practically a party for these people that have known each other a long time."

"Things get pretty dull for Brick — his recovery's so

slow," offered Carol, as if in explanation. " He likes people coming in."

" I'm sure he would," Henrietta murmured 'politely.

Paul wasn't finished. " I've done so much work in organizations around school where anybody, just anybody, who happened to be interested in student government or photography or whatever the project was had to be included. A setup like the Swingsters is a pleasure. Nobody was taken in unless we wanted him, all of us."

Jeff hoped he wasn't giving Paul the satisfaction of seeing his face redden. All the guy's words had had a carefully chosen sound. Spencer's Swingsters! One musical group Jeff Miles could be kept out of. Mr. Phillips might pressure Paul into putting up with somebody he didn't like in band and in quartet, but the Swingsters amounted also to a defiant answer to Mr. Phillips.

" Today has been nice," Henrietta was saying. " What about afternoons on Saturday or Sunday? You could come out to the ranch any time."

Jeff, not to be outdone in courtesy, added, " Or to our house."

" Either one would be fun," said Carol.

" Saturday afternoon is out for Swingsters," said Paul. " Our first engagement is the Pep Club dance Valentine's evening. Then there's the supper at Brick's next Sunday," he reminded Carol. " I shouldn't be surprised if we'd be tied up a good many week ends. Since the Swingsters are business, as well as something I really want to do, I feel they're entitled to first claim on my time."

Jeff was goaded to risk unsheathing his own claws a little, though hoping to avoid a direct clash before Mr. and Mrs. Hardesty. " I believe we have the picture pretty well in mind," he said. " All of us did agree, though, to give some time to this quartet work."

"True," agreed Paul, "but not social time. That's my point. I could put in an hour after school Tuesday and Friday afternoons."

For the time being, they left it at that.

Thinking it over, it seemed to Jeff that Paul, unable to get out of playing with the quartet, was determined to throw every block he could in the way of its success. And the quartet might have been successful, the way it started out. Might have reached that togetherness Mr. Hardesty spoke of as the essence of a musical organization. Only unity, harmony, didn't come simply from being a member of a musical group. The members, all of them, had to desire and develop it. In the quartet that wasn't so. It probably wouldn't accomplish anything.

After this conclusion Jeff was surprised to find during the next week that it did actually make a difference in band. Exactly how or why was hard to say.

Sometimes it was what Jeff thought of as pointing up. Having heard the piece simplified in its four basic parts, the quartet members knew the places where each should stand out. Then, in band, as you came to these passages, they pulled the stops and played it full. Others on a similar part evidently heard this and came along, so that the total effect had the right balance.

In other spots it was a question of timing. If you hit your note exactly on the two-and-a-half count, sort of catching the tune at the precise split second when it was tossed to you by the bass, "Paah-*oomp!* " the whole phrase went right. Missed, it was just notes. So you learned to listen and catch, and if others in the part were a trifle late, they picked it up on the next note. All this was a vague, psychological sort of thing, but the added zing it gave to a performance here and there could definitely be heard and felt. The spirit of the band began to pick up.

Mr. Phillips took official notice on the second Monday.

"We're justified now in going ahead with our plans for the Blossom Festival." Pleased smiles went back and forth, a spattering of applause. "I'd like to carry an official invitation, from the student body, the school principal, and the town of Garrison to the Music Educators' Conference."

"Like a letter?" Paul sprang to his feet. "I can get you those from student council and the principal. From the town I don't know — maybe I could see the mayor."

"What about the Chamber of Commerce? We were going to ask them for help," Walt Terry reminded him.

"Oh, sure. Well, who shall we have call on them?"

"You," laughed someone.

"Sylvia's dad is president," someone else remarked.

"It ought to be at a general meeting, I think," said Carol.

"That's right," Sylvia spoke up. "And it ought to be someone who could play for them. They're always looking for entertainment for their luncheons. Why not the quartet?"

The suggestion met with approval. Before Jeff knew it, he was scheduled to appear with the quartet at the Chamber of Commerce luncheon on the first Wednesday of February. This quartet certainly had a lot of unexpected angles.

In its next three rehearsals the quartet worked out two numbers for the luncheon. Then it was the day, and the four of them were excused from school midway during third hour.

They walked down the hill to the town hall, all Sundayed up, as Henrietta expressed it, under their winter coats. Four businessmen were waiting at the door to welcome them and take them to places at the head table. By a quarter past twelve nearly a hundred of Garrison's commercial leaders were seated in the big room.

Mr. Dodd kept the spirit of the meeting jovial. He ordered one man fined fifty cents for wearing a blue necktie. When another member made straight-faced protest, he was fined seventy-five cents for *not* wearing a blue necktie. This good-natured banter was new to the four students, but it helped them feel at ease.

Before dessert the quartet played " Stars of the Summer Night," with its rich harmony, and a spiritual called " Roll, Jordan, Roll," which featured some deep work for Paul on the bass. There was hearty applause.

"Now these young people have a matter of interest to present to us," Mr. Dodd announced. " I'll call on Paul Spencer, their president."

Paul had never, Jeff thought, used his nod, wink, and grin more winningly to advantage. He explained the possibilities of the music festival, how much it would mean to the school and the band — taking opportunity to thank Mr. Hardesty and the music committee for their support. He requested sponsorship of the festival by the group.

Jeff was surprised, therefore, when one of the men rose and said: " Mr. President, I'm sure this festival would be a fine thing for the school, and therefore for the community. No doubt all of us will want to co-operate in any way we can. But it really has no connection with business activity, so I don't see that it's exactly in order for us to sponsor it."

Another man rose. " Mr. President, you remember I volunteered, with you twisting my arm, to act as chairman of the Chamber's Cleanup-Paintup Campaign this spring. The dates of this festival come at the end of Cleanup-Paintup Week. Much as I wish the young folks luck with their project, I don't want you fellows getting tied up in something else and being too busy to help out on the campaign."

Jeff looked quickly at Paul. The head boy was fidgeting in his chair, flicking with a fingernail at the tablecloth, plainly taken aback. He was used to a student body that took his suggestions.

Mr. Dodd said: "How about that, Paul? We're behind the band. We want you to know that. Any way we could work this out?"

Paul got to his feet slowly. "Well, I don't know."

In an urgent undertone Jeff whispered, "Tell 'em about the parade."

Paul looked toward him blankly as though he had never before heard of a parade.

"Have an idea there, Jeff?" inquired Mr. Dodd. "Let's hear it. This," he reminded the assemblage, "is Jeff Miles, who plays that eu — you know what. The baritone."

Jeff rose, trying to sort his thoughts. He hadn't bargained for this. "As I understand it," he said, "there will be three or four hundred high school students in Garrison that Saturday and Sunday. They'll come from all the towns around here. Many of these musicians will be accompanied by their parents."

A chuckle arose, then two or three, and when the men saw that Jeff didn't realize the double meaning of what he'd said, there was a roar of hilarity that ended in hand clapping. When Jeff did catch on, he almost lost his original idea.

"Anyway," he said, "with lots of people in town, wouldn't it be good for business? I mean for sales and things? Like the gentleman there said, a connection with business activity."

He was putting this awkwardly, Jeff felt, but his words had stirred an exchange of glances and of remarks in undertone. The sound of the murmurs was approving.

"Then the other thing, about Cleanup-Paintup Week. What I was whispering was to remind Paul that the band and the student council had talked about a parade, maybe a week before the festival, to promote the idea. Publicity."

He looked toward Paul. The head boy was sitting set-faced. Well, he'd fumbled the ball himself!

"What I thought," Jeff continued, "was that the parade could be a starter for Cleanup-Paintup Week too. Business houses might have floats advertising Cleanup-Paintup, and the student organizations could do their stunts for the festival, and the band would furnish the music. It all sort of goes together in my mind."

Applause was hearty as he sat down. In only a moment the Chamber of Commerce had voted to cosponsor, with the high school band, the proposed regional music festival. The meeting adjourned, and the quartet members gathered up their instruments to return to school.

Paul, under cover of the general movement, said, low-voiced, "Well, you managed to sell your parade, didn't you?"

"What were you selling them?" Jeff retorted.

Without waiting for a reply he stepped up beside Henrietta for the walk back, leaving Paul and Carol to follow. There was nothing to be accomplished by a row. Besides, they were both still under their pledge to work together.

At rehearsal next day Mr. Phillips announced: "I think we can count on having the festival. The quartet got us the sponsorship of the Chamber of Commerce. Now, until the invitation is accepted by the Music Educators' Conference, we have nothing more to do, except learn fifteen pages of music till you can play 'em with your hands tied behind you while standing on your head in a six-foot snowbank! Take 'Under the Double Eagle' to warm up."

That set the tone of every rehearsal for weeks.

When Jeff arrived home, Dad was visiting in the living room with two men.

"Jeff, meet Mr. Finnegan," he said, "and Mr. Finnegan. Earl and Vince. The Mule Ear has a crew."

They shook hands with Jeff, dark, heavy-set men dressed in worn but sturdy clothes of miners. Jeff noticed a twinkle of humor in their eyes. He recognized, and shared, the quiet elation that had been in Dad's tone.

The Finnegans stayed for dinner. Certainly they seemed cut to a different pattern from Windy Farnum. They had, it came out, a mine of their own that they were trying to develop.

"Finnegan's Wake, it's called," said Earl, with a quizzical half-smile.

"Sorrow! Sorrow! Sorrow!" Vince added whimsically. "Nothing, you understand, that a few paltry dollars wouldn't remedy. Meaning, we're broke."

"And mighty glad to find work in our line, so that we can accumulate a little money to go back up and sink to no avail in the Wake."

When, on Saturday, Jeff went up to the Mule Ear to help, he understood Dad's enthusiasm for the Finnegan brothers. There was nothing about a mine that Earl and Vince couldn't do the same as Dad and Tony. The four experienced men moved smoothly about the workings, never wasting a motion, never getting in each other's way despite the cramped space. Things at the Mule Ear at last were looking up.

Strangely enough, that posed a new challenge to Jeff, one

that anybody else would have found hard, perhaps, to understand. The Finnegans made it seem more likely that the Mule Ear venture would turn out successfully and increased, in a way, the probability that the Mileses would stay in Garrison permanently.

Jeff wanted to stay permanently. Yet the prospect brought home to him what had not come out of his experience before: when you were permanent in a place, your problems were permanent too.

It was quite possible that he might be stuck, indefinitely, with Paul Spencer and his circle of cronies who regarded Jeff with chill eyes. He might always face the solid front of a clique who considered themselves Garrison High, and anybody not born here a fugitive from justice.

That was the rub. The folks were establishing him here, but so far he hadn't managed to do much that made him belong. He wasn't establishing himself. His only achievement was membership in the band. The band was where he'd have to work it out. This Blossom Festival — that was something to take hold of. He vowed he'd give the festival everything he had.

It had become crucially important to him.

CHAPTER 10

O<small>N THE</small> T<small>HURSDAY</small> and Friday Mr. Phillips would be away at the Music Educators' Conference, the band was to be directed by Paul Spencer.

The announcement almost bowled Jeff over. Yet it was logical enough. Paul was president of the band. He regularly conducted the tune-up. No mention was made of Paul's leadership of Spencer's Swingsters, but Jeff had heard the girls say that the music for the Pep Club dance had been O.K. and Paul — on the same authority — really cute.

He would be. Nobody Jeff had ever seen was better at playing to the galleries. But Jeff was not gallery, and what might happen when he was placed under Paul's control was hard to tell.

Mr. Phillips solemnly warned the group that any punk who got out of line during his absence could expect slow death by the thumbs on his return. Then he gave his dry grin and they laughed. Jeff didn't laugh. Suppose Paul took advantage of the occasion to find, and report, Jeff Miles out of line?

To begin his reign, Paul mounted the stand with his sousaphone and called, "'Officer of the Day.'" A howl greeted this.

"Gonna start tough, hunh?"

"Who d'you think we are? Goldman's bunch?"

"I can't do it! I just never can get it right!"

Paul was laughing with them. It was as simple a number as they had. "Come on, now, kids," he made rejoinder. "Let us have no loafing. Be strong. Be brave. Be quiet, will you?"

He tapped loudly with his foot to set the rhythm and hit the first note with them. They blared away gleefully. When they had finished, he asked, "What do you want next?"

"'Military Escort.'"

"O.K. 'Military Escort' it is." That set the pattern of Paul's conducting. Anything to please, and the more they were pleased, the more Paul loved it. They played all the arrangements of popular tunes that they had, and filled in with easy marches.

When anyone got to talking too loudly, Paul would say: "Hey, guys, break it up, will you? Don't get me in bad." The plea was always accompanied by the nod, wink, and grin, and order was always restored. In fact, there was remarkably little disturbance during the whole of the time, however little was accomplished musically.

Jeff took care to keep himself inconspicuous, and Paul took no notice of him whatever. Whether the guy had more sportsmanship than Jeff suspected, or didn't dare single Jeff out alone to be reported out of line, or simply enjoyed so thoroughly occupying the spotlight position uncontested that he forgot his grudge, Jeff never knew. At any rate, the two days passed without incident.

When Friday's band period was over, Jeff and Henrietta went up to get set for quartet rehearsal, as usual.

"Can't make it tonight, folks," Paul announced. "The Swingsters are playing a job this evening at a schoolhouse down toward Fielding, and we have to get going. Can't ignore the old play-for-pay angle."

143

If a guy needed dough, what could you say? That it was less than an hour's trip to Fielding? Maybe Paul needed a break between school and work; nobody can go at top speed all the time. The fact remained when his schedule had become such that something had to give, it was the school band, through the quartet, that gave. Prospects for the school band didn't look good if its leader couldn't hold up his end.

With Mr. Phillips' return, the school principal came in. He wanted to commend the band for its ability to carry on. Also he had an announcement.

"You all know how well our basketball team has done this year. As of now they have won seventeen and lost four. If they win their last game, against Eagle City next Saturday, they will tie Eagle City for second place in the conference and have a chance through play-offs to get in the state tournament. Since this is such an important game, we'd like to take the band to Eagle City if you want to go."

The response left no doubt that they wanted to go.

"We'll have two buses for you," the principal said then. "I know it's a short trip, but Eagle Pass makes it a difficult one, and we'd like to have as few student-driven cars as possible on that road at night. We have traffic hazards very much in mind this year." They sobered quickly at that. "I'll ask that all band members go in the buses rather than by car."

When the principal had left, Mr. Phillips said: "Before this came up, I was going to tell you that our bid for a music festival was accepted, and the official notice will be along in a few days. Now I guess I'd better not tell you." Laughter. "Anyway, we'll wait until next Monday, after this trip is over, to select our committee and get to work on festival plans."

144

All week Jeff looked forward to that bus trip. His uniform pressed and his horn polished, he was at the school promptly at six thirty Saturday night. The two ponderous, forty-passenger buses were already drawn up to the curb, motors idling, drivers leaning against a front fender. The black letters of GARRISON CENTRALIZED SCHOOL DISTRICT and of various caution signs stood out boldly against their yellow paint.

Mr. Phillips said, " Give me a hand, Jeff? "

The sousaphones and drums were to be loaded. Jeff helped Mr. Phillips pack the instruments in the first three seats on each side and strap them against shifting on turns.

" The guys and gals always want to sit as far back as possible," Mr. Phillips observed. " Don't ask me why. It rides much rougher in the rear."

Jeff chuckled. By now the members had gathered and Rosie had completed a noisy taking of the roll. They began swarming into the buses.

Paul was in the crowd that entered Jeff's bus with Carol and Mel and Virgie and Walt. Paul took immediate charge of the seating: " Oh, this'll do . . . Here, gal . . . There's a seat, Walt." Jeff debated whether to get out and go up to the front bus. Mr. Phillips stepped in beside the driver.

" All set in here? " he called generally.

Voices called, " All set."

" Jeff," said the director, " someone needs to occupy this single seat across from the driver, to keep an eye on the instruments."

" O.K.," said Jeff, and took the seat designated.

" I'm lettin' the other bus get half a mile ahead," the driver volunteered to Jeff across the aisle. " Don't slow up traffic so much that way."

He was an elderly man whom Jeff recognized as a custodian at the school. " My name's Collins," he added. " Got three children of my own, all older'n you."

Evidently he wanted to talk. Jeff accepted the offer. Conversation was going at half-shout level in the rear two thirds of the bus, centering around Paul. Talking with Mr. Collins was better than sitting in solitude.

One of Mr. Collins' daughters was musical. Piano. He'd used to dabble some in mining. Too uncertain for him. He'd had the flu last week, and was sure glad to get back on solid food. The bus packed a hundred and fifty horsepower in its six-cylinder motor, and had four speeds forward. In that compound low she'd blame near climb a tree.

After the first five miles these morsels began to be tossed out more slowly. The highway had left the easy course of the Rio del Oro and started to climb Eagle Pass. Mr. Collins was busy with the gearshift as they wound back and forth up the side of a narrow canyon in a series of sharp hairpin turns. Looking down, and down, and down, to where the lights of cars just starting up appeared to be fireflies, Jeff could understand why the principal had urged that no students drive this road at night if it could be avoided.

The bus's progress was laboriously slow, but at last they topped out in the wide saddle of Eagle Pass, crossing the mighty backbone of North America. Upward at each side of the highway the slopes rose bald and shadowy in the faint light, towering above timber line.

Then they made cautious descent of the equally spectacular western side, Mr. Collins driving in second gear or first. The bus popped and banged with backfire, and Paul was moved to recite " The Shooting of Dan McGrew."

The confines of the Eagle City gym bulged with the crowd. The band was packed in until the trombones had to tilt their instruments upward to keep slides from bump-

146

ing players in front. They played, on Mr. Phillips' order, at half volume, but the small space still rocked with the noise.

Many of the crowd stood, for numerous rooters from Garrison had made the trip, and Eagle City was out in force. Among the people Jeff saw Brick Lassiter. He had discarded his crutch and used a cane on the side of the leg in the cast, and he no longer wore a sling. Once he waved briefly in the direction of the band, but when Mr. Phillips looked his way, he scowled and turned his head. The heavy-shouldered, florid-faced man on one side of Brick and a rather large, tired-looking lady on the other Jeff guessed were Brick's parents.

The Garrison Warriors played their hearts out that evening against an Eagle City team too tall and too sharp of eye. It was close, but Garrison had to be content with third place in the league, and there would be no play-offs. At the end the band stayed in their seats to play "Fight On, Fight On, for Garrison," in stanch tribute to the team's valiant effort.

Then Mr. Phillips called, "To save confusion, will each of you take the same bus going back?" Jeff again took the single seat opposite the driver, while Paul and company assembled toward the rear.

The crowd were subdued as they started home, tired, and disappointed at the game's outcome. There were some halfhearted efforts at singing as they climbed the pass, but most folks had used up their voices in cheering.

"Wish they hadn't had that daggone refreshment booth out in the hall," Mr. Collins remarked to Jeff, "or that I'd had sense to pass up the hot dogs and Cokes. Don't set well, this time o' night."

"I wanted some," Jeff replied, "but right after eating my lip is not so good on the horn."

147

Mr. Collins complained of discomfort two or three times. As they neared the top of the pass Paul got going on " Casey at the Bat." Jeff turned that way to listen, and forgot about Mr. Collins and his stomach-ache.

"Oh, somewhere in this . . ."

Jeff straightened suddenly. The bus had veered sharply, then swerved sharply back. Its speed increased. Jeff looked across at Mr. Collins questioningly.

The bus driver was slumped forward and to the side, half against the wall of the bus and half on the wheel. His head swayed limply. Unconscious!

" Hey! " Jeff yelled at the top of his lungs, and leaped.

He got hold of the wheel and swung it over barely in time to keep them from going over the side of that bottomless drop. He flung himself against Mr. Collins to get a precarious perch on the edge of the seat. He stabbed with his foot for the brake.

Mr. Collins had not, Jeff realized, shifted gears. The tremendous weight was rolling in high down a grade so steep even second gear would have been dangerous. Jeff found the pedal and shoved.

The bus lurched sickeningly. Jeff fought the wheel. A scream shrilled out high. A car grinding up the grade toward them honked in protest.

Then Jeff remembered. Make a fast stop by jerks. He jabbed at the brake with repeated short plunges. The bus slowed rapidly.

He couldn't reach the clutch. He switched off the ignition, groped with one hand for the emergency brake, and steered with the other. Too many things to do at once. Behind him was an uproar of terrified screams and shouts and yells.

The speedometer needle dropped to zero, and Jeff realized they had stopped. With an effort he unclenched his aching hand from the wheel.

"What the heck's going on, Miles?"

"Mr. Collins," Jeff answered weakly. "He passed out!"

Several of them got Mr. Collins out of his twisted position and stretched him on the floor. The old man was breathing heavily, giving little unconscious moans of pain.

"Get him outside in the air," Paul ordered.

Jeff pushed the door lever.

"It's cold out there," said someone. "March wind."

"You have to keep an unconscious person warm," one of the girls said.

"What we need is a doctor," said Carol, "and quick!"

"All the cars going back to Garrison passed us on the climb." Jeff sweated. "And the other bus is ahead. We can't expect help."

"Can you drive the bus, Jeff?" Virgie Sullivan asked.

"I don't know. I drive my dad's truck."

"You got it stopped," said Carol.

Jeff climbed in the driver's seat and got the motor going again while numerous hands lifted Mr. Collins to the long bench at the very back of the bus. He regained consciousness long enough to gasp, "Oh, my chest!" Then he fainted again.

"They always keep a first-aid kit in the glove compartment of the bus," said someone, "but I wouldn't know what to give him."

"Get him to a doctor," Carol repeated.

Jeff pulled the door lever and called, "Hang on!"

He shifted into low and started creeping down the grade, the precipice at the side crowding his mind. Mr. Collins groaned.

"Can't you hurry?" urged somebody.

Warily, Jeff shifted to second. They picked up speed. He steered with a grim concentration that seemed to squeeze him in iron bands. The bus handled not too much unlike the truck that hauled supplies to the Mule Ear.

They went faster than he would have liked, yet maddeningly slow when he heard the sick man's moaning. A car passed them. If there'd been any way to get its attention, the car's occupants might have helped.

As they came, at long last, off the pass and onto the easier highway, another car passed them.

"Hey!" shouted Jeff. "That's a Highway Patrol!"

"Blink your lights!" yelled Paul.

Jeff not only did that, frantically, but he leaned on the bus's horn button. The white car with the tall radio aerial slowed, hesitated, and stopped. Jeff breathed hard in relief.

"What's the deal?" asked the officer, leaning his gray-uniformed figure in the door.

They got him told, trying not to talk all at once. He went back to look at Mr. Collins.

"You're right," he said, straightening. "This is no case for first aid; this is for the hospital in Garrison. You seem to be driving all right, kid. Afraid to let your foot down?"

"Not too much now," Jeff answered. "That pass about scared me to death."

"It's fairly level and fairly straight now," said the officer, "and not much over five miles. You get on my taillight and give 'er everything you've got. I'll clear the way with my siren."

He ran back to the patrol car and was pulling out before Jeff had time to be panicked. He shifted, and shifted again, and again. The lumbering vehicle began to pick up speed.

Then they were tearing through the night, every light on at its brightest, swerving past cars that pulled to the side of the highway at the shriek of the patrolman's siren. The kids behind were shouting again, but Jeff scarcely heard them. He kept his right foot shoved hard down and clung to the steering wheel with every ounce of his strength, feeling the awful sway of the bus with each small turn, no matter how wide he took the curves in utter disregard of traffic lanes.

The speedometer needle kept going up. Jeff didn't dare to look. He was tied in a hall of blackness with nothing but the wide white wedge of his headlights and the red wink of the patrol car ahead, and the endless, chilling shriek wailing back over him.

Buildings loomed and streaked past on either side and he lifted his foot. They were in Garrison. When their speed died to twenty-five, Jeff shifted to second and rammed down the accelerator again. He lurched into a driveway and hit the brakes. They slowed to a stop at the ambulance entrance to the Garrison hospital.

The patrolman appeared at the bus door again, followed by two men in white. They got Mr. Collins onto a stretcher and out the bus door into the building. The band members, Jeff included, sat where they were, some of them chattering in low, tense voices. Jeff was too numb even to think.

The patrolman appeared once more. "Five and three tenths miles in four minutes and forty seconds. I didn't ask to see your driver's license, but you're all right, son. I'll need your name, and so forth, for my report."

Jeff reached for his billfold, where he carried his driver's license. It was steadying, somehow, to deal in dry facts for a few minutes while the patrolman wrote in his book.

Finished with that, Jeff asked, "When can we find out how it is with Mr. Collins?"

"Let's go see," suggested the other.

They went into the building, and after a short wait a desk attendant reported: "He's resting easier. He's under oxygen now."

Back outside, they gave the other students the report.

"Was it acute indigestion or a heart attack or what?" Carol asked.

"They probably won't have it diagnosed until they've run tests."

"Maybe he couldn't take that altitude after his sickness last week."

The officer told Jeff, "I'll stick with you until you get over to the school."

Jeff tooled the big machine carefully through the darkened streets of Garrison and drew up behind the other bus. At sight of the patrol car, Mr. Phillips came running.

"What — Where's Collins?" he demanded as he saw Jeff at the wheel.

Something in the director's familiar presence seemed to release abruptly the pent-up tension in all of them. They tumbled out and surrounded him, everybody giving his own excited account of what had taken place. How Jeff had seen the emergency; how Jeff had stopped the bus; how Jeff had driven on; how Jeff had got the attention of the patrolman. Jeff wouldn't have heard his name so many times ordinarily in a year.

"You remember you assigned Miles to that single seat," Paul said at last. "That's how he happened to be the one involved."

"It's lucky," observed the patrolman, "that he also happened to be a guy with a cool head and a quick one. Come on, kid; I'll drive you home."

That was all right with Jeff. All he wanted at the moment was to get home and see if Mom had left a snack out for him. Then he wanted to sleep till about tomorrow noon.

He was doing all right with sleep when a knock sounded on his bedroom door. He rolled over crossly and mumbled, "Hunh?" His clock pointed to eight thirty.

Ginny's voice called: "Are you awake? What's this supercilious thing the reporters want to see you about?"

"What's who want to see me?" Jeff demanded with extraordinary clarity.

"Reporters from the Garrison *Monitor*. They're on their way over here right now. You'd better get dressed."

Coming awake, Jeff grabbed for his clothes. He washed his face, combed his hair and decided that since he'd shaved yesterday — Jeff arrived at the foot of the stairs as Dad ushered in two men in topcoats. One of them carried a Speed Graphic.

"Could we have a picture?" the one with the camera asked. "Just stand right there."

Jeff was too surprised to do anything else.

Dad remarked, "It looks as if last night was one time when we should have waited up for you."

Jeff grinned at him. The camera flash bulb flared. The other man took folded copy paper from his pocket. "How did you happen to notice that Mr. Collins had lost consciousness?"

"Corn's sake!" exclaimed Jeff.

The interview was detailed. How far did he think the bus rolled before he got it under control? How close to the edge did he estimate they were when he first reached the wheel? How long did he think it took them to get off the pass? And so on and on and on.

Jeff explained as best he could, attempting at the same time to give his astonished parents some idea of the whole incident.

When at last the newspapermen left, Ginny said: " I shall cook you flapjacks and two boiled eggs with my own lily-white hands. Your favorite breakfast. We've got a supercilious hero in the house! "

By way of reply Jeff could do no better than a feeble, " For corn's sake! "

Mr. Phillips phoned to ask how he was feeling and Dr. Price, Mel's father, dropped by and praised him for getting the patient to medical aid. After church the Hardestys stopped in, all four of them. That especially pleased Jeff. Still later in the day the school principal called and said warm words to his father and mother.

Next morning the paper carried bold headlines: " GARRISON HIGH STUDENT AVERTS TRAGEDY." And his own mug, as Ginny put it, grinned out from the middle two columns.

Before Jeff reached school, students were calling, " Nice work, Miles; good going, fellow." Students whose names he didn't even know. The same thing continued after he entered the building. Friendly greetings reached him from Senior Circle itself.

In the middle of American history class Mrs. Ickes, the stately, white-haired teacher, said, " Jeff, you're wanted in the hall."

Out there a wondering Jeff found the editor and a reporter of the *Garrison High Times*. Though he tried to make it as brief as possible, he had to give the story all over again. The thing was snowballing too much.

In band, when roll was taken, Mr. Phillips said: " None of my students ever before had a bus ride like the one Saturday night, and I trust they never will again. I'm just thankful it all turned out so fortunately. Now let's move on to specific arrangements for the Blossom Festival."

That suited Jeff. The bus thing had been accidental, might have happened to anybody. The satisfaction it gave him was not the substantial sort that comes from planning out something and working to accomplish it. This Blossom Festival — he'd really like to have a part in that. Anything you could do on such a project would give credit you could feel was truly earned.

"I suppose — " Paul was presiding from the stand " — the first thing to do is to elect a general chairman. Then we could set up committees to handle different parts of the work. Is that O.K. by everybody?" Apparently it was. "Then nominations are open for general chairman of the Blossom Festival."

Walt Terry, who was trap drummer for Spencer's Swingsters, promptly said: "You. I mean I nominate Paul Spencer."

There, Jeff thought, went his fine hopes for the Blossom Festival. It was to be a closed-corporation affair, as he should have foreseen. Paul and Paul's friends!

Unexpectedly, Mr. Phillips' drawl came from the side of the room. "I never interfere in student elections, but Paul, as president of the student body and of the band, is going to have plenty to do acting as official host, welcoming guests, serving as master of ceremonies — all that. I think someone else should have this responsibility."

"I withdraw my nomination," Walt said dutifully.

Paul flashed his nod, wink, and grin at Walt and repeated whimsically, "Nominations are open for general chairman of the Blossom Festival."

Bill Hayes got to his feet. "I'd like to nominate Jeff Miles."

Jeff straightened in astonishment. What — Maybe Bill had it in mind to square up for what he'd said about the solo in " Poet and Peasant." Bill didn't have to do that.

Rosie turned from the board, where she had written " Jeff Miles." " Candidates withdraw," she stated. When Jeff looked blank, she added: " Get out of the room, you big lug. It's a custom here."

There was good-natured laughter as Jeff started for the door. The unexpected was coming his way too frequently of late. He went across the gallery and leaned over the railing to watch the gym class below do calisthenics.

He wondered who else would be nominated and come out to join him. Maybe Walt. The regulars would surely have somebody. His own nomination he recognized as a courtesy.

" You can come back now." Paul Spencer was speaking from the band room door.

Jeff recrossed the gallery. Now what? Had they called the election off, or something?

As he passed Paul, the head boy muttered under his breath: " So the publicity paid off. Nice timing! "

Jeff didn't get it. He started toward his place beside Mel, wondering about it.

" Unanimous ballot." Rosie's parade-ground voice carried into his consciousness. " Jeff Miles is general chairman of the Blossom Festival."

Jeff stumbled and almost went flat on his amazed face. Somebody among the second trumpets gave him a push, and the next thing he was up to the stand. Applause went around.

" Corn's sake! " Jeff stammered. " What do I do now? "

They laughed, and somebody yelled, " Speech! " But Dick raised his oboe and suggested, " Get somebody to take charge of the food."

That opened a line of thinking to Jeff. " First we need

somebody to plan the time, don't we? A committee to set up the events? Schedule committee. Nominations are open for chairman of the schedule committee."

Henrietta was elected to that job.

"This could take forever," said Jeff. "How's if we let each chairman pick the other members of the committee?"

That was made a motion and passed. Then Dick, by voters' logic, was made chairman of the food committee. They thought two people would be needed for housing — finding homes in the town that would entertain one or more visiting students overnight. Carol was elected chairman of girls' housing, and Mel of boys' housing. There ought to be a special committee for the dance, the big social event of the festival, the Blossom Ball. Rosie Mahoney got that job, defeating Sylvia Dodd and Peggy Sweet in a close vote.

The thing began to be real in Jeff's mind. He'd wanted to work on the Blossom Festival. Cheese! Here he was in a key spot! This could be big, the biggest thing that'd ever happened to him.

"Could the six of us meet," he asked, "say Wednesday night at my house? That would give time to pick your committee members and we could start work. I'd like to get going on this."

"O.K. by me."

"Wednesday's good."

"I'll stay in town with my aunt," agreed Henrietta.

"Can you be there, Mr. Phillips?" Jeff wanted to know, and the director nodded.

Jeff stepped down. He couldn't remember when he'd been so excited. He'd never dreamed of having the leadership. Any leadership.

He glanced toward Paul, sitting among the sousaphones. *So the publicity paid off. Nice timing!* Jeff understood the

157

remark now. The horned monarch of the band had a rival, another leader in that treasured spot front-and-center.

So what would happen? Would Paul battle for his supremacy? Run down every suggestion, sneer at every effort, belittle the whole festival in the eyes of his following? Surely he wouldn't dare. The success of the school year meant too much to him as head boy. He wouldn't.

Or, Jeff wondered, would he?

CHAPTER 11

"I T's SWELL," said Ginny as she dusted the coffee table,
"that you're a big wheel now, but you make a supercilious
lot of work."

"One committee job and I'm a big wheel!" Jeff scoffed.

"One committee meeting, and your back is broken."

"Not only do I have to dust all the furniture an extra
time, but I'll have to stay up till all hours to help serve sand-
wiches and Cokes."

"I'll lug tables or something when you have your Girl
Scout troop meeting," Jeff promised. "Now will you beat
it so I can get this list of things to do made out?"

"Sisters are a sorry lot!" muttered the girl, departing.

Jeff grinned after her bustling figure. Actually, she was
getting a considerable honk out of this; gatherings of kids
at the Miles home had not, through the years, been as common a thing as they both had wished. Ginny simply had to
keep him reminded of what an important part in the pro-
ceedings she filled.

Shortly after seven Mr. Phillips arrived with a brief case
of bulletins, memoranda, and letters. Already the director
was in communication with the people from neighboring
states who would serve as judges and award ratings.

Instead of having to call the meeting to order and proceed

formally, Jeff found Henrietta, Dick, Carol, Mel, and Rosie becoming involved in discussion as they arrived. The hopping around from one subject to another disturbed him a bit at first. He had a carefully planned list of things to take up in order. But ideas spilled out with such rapid give-and-take that he forgot about the list and concentrated on keeping up with the kids' thinking.

At last they got a schedule of events set up, subject to Henrietta's committee being able to reserve the times and places. Chairmen listed committee members with Jeff. Dick agreed to work with the Chamber of Commerce officers on food, for they were counting on that body to finance much of the cost of the three meals to be furnished. Mr. Phillips produced a statement from the school treasurer of the amount of money in the band's festival fund, and they set to work to divide it up.

" I suppose the thing to do," Jeff suggested, " is to put the most money on the most important things. Brainy idea, isn't it? "

" What stood out for me last year," Carol remembered, " were the big dance Saturday night and staying as a guest of one of the girls afterward. Sounds as if I didn't take the music very seriously, Mr. Phillips."

" I agree," said Mr. Phillips. " Surprised? " He laughed. " We think the best outcomes of festivals are the associations and the exchange of ideas. That's the reason we don't have contests much any more."

" Yay-hey," said Rosie. " Then can I have the biggest hunk of budget for the dance? I have a snorky idea: fix up the gym real flossy, *and* — " she paused impressively " — hire an honest-to-goodness top-notch professional dance band to play."

" Oh, wouldn't that be tony! "

"So much better than canned music. Make it a really big-time prom."

"Do you know Mr. Oliver at Parkville?" Rosie asked Mr. Phillips. "He has that band called Oliver's Octet that's really smooth. I wish we could get them."

"I know of him," nodded Mr. Phillips. "He's getting quite a reputation. Plays all over the region. I shouldn't be surprised that for a school group he might make a special rate and take the job, if his schedule isn't too crowded."

"It wouldn't do any harm to write and ask," Rosie decided. "There's plenty of time. How much money do we get?"

They allotted the Blossom Ball Committee the lion's share of the budget, for everyone agreed that having Oliver's Octet for the ball would give more prestige to the festival than anything else they could do.

Housing was the next big problem.

"Carol and I each have on our committee one student who's pretty good in art," Mel said. "We had in mind to put posters in all the store windows asking people to entertain visiting band members in their homes. Even so, it's going to be an order, getting enough rooms."

"We need," added Carol, "some sort of terrific sales campaign. I wonder if a lot of the placards and stunts in the Cleanup-Paintup parade couldn't be on that subject."

"Corn's sake! What about that parade? Who's going to take charge of it?"

They pondered that.

"We need another chairman," Mr. Phillips suggested. "Jeff has his hands full, and Henrietta already has enough schedules to arrange."

Dick said: "Paul's the logical one for that job, since all the organizations in school are invited to enter the parade and Paul is president of the student council. He's good at things like contacting the business people and getting them to enter floats."

" Mr. Phillips wanted to keep Paul free for general host," somebody recalled.

" The parade will be over a week before there's any festival to host," Henrietta pointed out. " Paul's the person to get across the idea that it'd be a fine thing for people to take in a visiting bandsman or two, or six, for Saturday night and breakfast Sunday."

That seemed to bring the meeting to a conclusion, with nothing settled about the parade. Ginny was a question mark in the doorway to the kitchen. Jeff gave the word for her and Mom to bring on the refreshments.

While the committee ate, Jeff played some of his choicest Edwin Franko Goldman band records. Talk and laughter echoed through the big house, setting up a warm glow in him. This evening marked a turning point — the first real get-together of Garrison young people in his home.

Later, as he thought over the parade, it occurred to him that maybe it was a smart idea to ask Paul to take charge of it. The kids had no doubt Paul could do it well, and he could if he wanted to. It might be a way of showing Paul his help would be appreciated and of getting him to use his influence to build up the festival.

After school next day, as the band room cleared, Jeff said, " Paul, got a minute? " Mr. Phillips had taken off for the school office. They would have the room to themselves.

" A minute for what? " Paul demanded.

Jeff put it carefully. " We need somebody to take charge of the Cleanup-Paintup parade. Since different school organizations will be taking part, the committee thought you, as president of the student body . ." The look on Paul's face caused Jeff to let the sentence trail.

" So you're going to cram that parade down my throat or blow a gasket trying! "

" Now wait a minute! " The violence of Paul's feelings had a way of catching Jeff unprepared.

" You're not getting *me* to flunky for you! "

Jeff felt his temper slipping. " All right, skip it. I'm not after anybody to flunky for me."

" Not much! All you want is somebody to do the work on your ideas while you take the credit and get your picture in the paper. O.K., you like being a hero, you like running things — now run 'em! Show everybody what a big shot you are."

Jeff's temper went overboard. " If you think this job's so big, why didn't you get on it three months ago instead of putting in all your time on something that sucks off from band and puts it second place to your own outfit? "

Paul's voice shook. " You can afford to put your soul into it. Band's what's building you up, and you don't have to think about anything else."

Jeff got himself under control. A fight wouldn't settle any of this. It went too deep, was too bitter. At this moment all the ill will that had been gathering between them this whole year was ready to spill. It ought to spill, he thought. Curiously, the thought calmed him. This was it. He reached for a chair.

" We might as well have this out," he said, " while I'm sitting down with my hands in my pockets. What is it you've got against me? Ever since the first day I came to Garrison — "

" Ever since," Paul half shouted, " you've done nothing but scheme and maneuver to grab glory! Impress people with your car, and your high-class home on The Hill, and the traveling you've done, and the big schools you've attended, and your big-time ideas! Sure, the local yokels were supposed to roll over and wave their paws in the air when *you* showed up. You're big stuff. It's no matter about a guy that's worked for the school for years, taken the lead, made things go."

"Why'd you quit?" cut in Jeff. "You haven't taken any lead in this. You didn't even take an interest, it seems to me, and the Blossom Festival could be a big deal."

"You'll make it a big deal for you, of course. If I wasn't head boy I'd tell you and everybody else to take this Blossom Festival and shove it in the first badger burrow."

"Why don't you?"

"Only because I hope that after you get through using it to blow yourself up, there may still be something left that I can save to serve the interests of the school."

"What interests of the school?" Jeff demanded. "Spencer's Swingsters? Anyway, is working to make it a good festival, if *I* do it, blowing myself up?"

"I said go ahead," Paul retorted. "Run it your way. But I'm not working for you."

"This is getting us no place." Jeff rose and picked up his horn. "Just understand this: don't you and your bunch dream up any funny ideas you're going to plug things. The first guy — or dozen — that gets in the way of the Blossom Festival I'll clear out personally."

Sick inside, Jeff strode out and made his way home. It hadn't been a good, clean fight that got it out of your system so that you could shake hands afterward and forget it. Something about this was ugly and festering.

Jeff was so snappish around the house, and ate with such unusual moderation, that Mom began to get her concerned look and Dad to eye him speculatively. So finally, after

Ginny had gone upstairs, he told them, trying to be honest. There was no sense bringing it to them if all he wanted was a whitewash job.

" So that's the way it's gone," he finished. " I still don't get it. Why me? He's the type that likes everybody — everybody else."

Dad, in his easy chair, squinted through the smoke of his pipe. " Maybe," he drawled, " you should ask, ' Why Paul?' "

" What? " Jeff didn't get that.

Dad asked. " What's there in Paul to make him the one that is particularly allergic to you? "

Jeff hadn't thought of it from that angle. In fairness he had to say: " There's the rest of his crowd too. A bunch of big wheels that stick together."

" Isn't Carol a big wheel? " asked Mom. " And the Price boy? "

" I suppose so. Certainly Carol. And Mel runs around with 'em. But *they* don't seem to think much about being big wheels."

" Ah! " said Dad. " Evidently Paul does think about being a big wheel. Maybe too much. Could it be his position as Head Everything is so important to him that he lives in constant dread of losing it? "

" To me? " Jeff scoffed.

" Probably he'd *say* that was ridiculous too," smiled Mom. " But I think what Dad's talking about is one of those feelings that are way down underneath. An almost instinctive fear of anyone else who becomes too prominent."

" Oh, this goes back long before the bus thing," Jeff explained. " That first Saturday, when I took some kids home, he says I did it to impress people with my car."

" What kind of car does he drive? " Dad inquired.

"They don't have a car; maybe can't afford it. Paul's father is dead and his mother is an operator or something for the telephone company."

"But you get to drive a car, such as it is," Dad grinned.

"Also you have a dad," added Mom.

"Also such as *he* is," Dad caught it up. "And plenty of money — that's always something the other fellow has. You begin to get the pitch, Jeff?"

"Hanged if I do! Most of the guys he runs around with have dads and cars, homes, all that."

"He made some crack about your home?" Dad inquired.

"Yes. 'High-class home on The Hill,'" Jeff quoted.

Dad nodded. "Practically next door to the girl he dates, too, whether he mentioned that or not. He has no way of knowing it's the first permanent home you've ever had. Where do he and his mother live?"

"Down on Main, three hundred block. I think it's one of those flats above the Garrison Laundry. But what does that have to do with it? Brick Lassiter has about the flossiest home in town and a dad who's wealthy and his own car . . . or did have his own car."

"Brick will follow Paul," Mom put in. "You won't."

"You have everything," Dad summed it up.

"What!"

"From his point of view," Dad added. "That's what you have to see to understand this. Nothing in your point of view explains it. I'll bet that to Paul you look like Mr. Man-of-the-World. Mr. Got-Rocks, a fellow who's on the make, until before long you'll eclipse his sun. He stands to lose everything that means most to him if he doesn't stop you cold."

"There's only one way to do that," Mom carried on. "Shut you out. Let you know his friends won't be your friends unless he says so. The more ability you display, the more he has to show you."

" Show me what? " Jeff asked, still bewildered.

" That he's a better man than you are," said Mom.

" Because he's terribly scared he isn't," said Dad.

" Paul Spencer? The way he rates? " Jeff couldn't believe it. " You saw him at Parkville. He's like that every chance he gets. If ever a guy was good, and knows it, it's Paul."

" I'm not impressed," said Dad. " I've seen men who had to keep constantly showing how good they were. Underneath I suspect you'd find Paul haunted by a desperate fear that if the truth were known he hasn't got what it takes, and that you have more of solid ability."

" Corn's sake! " This was all too much for Jeff. " But what do I do? "

Dad looked at Mom. " I was afraid that would come up."

" You could start taking his hostility for no more than it's worth," Mom suggested. " Try not to let him upset you, knowing he can't help being the way he is."

" Keep out of his way," offered Dad.

Jeff said: " That I can't. The quartet has to stay together on account of the rest of the band and even play the *Rigoletto* number at the festival."

After a moment's reflection Dad mused: " I think I see Phillips' point. Both of you are needed by the band and the school. The quartet makes one thing you have in common, one thing to draw you together."

" In other words," said Mom, " Mr. Phillips is hoping each of you may be of big enough caliber to lay aside your personal feelings during the time necessary to work for a cause you both believe in, even if you come to blows immediately after. That's been done. It makes things a bit hopeful."

167

"I don't see how," gloomed Jeff.

"Holds it open," Dad explained, "in case something should happen to change Paul's attitude."

"What could happen," Jeff wanted to know, "unless I changed his face around for him?"

"It's not his face you don't like," Mom said. "A person like Paul sometimes straightens out if he gets himself on what he feels is solid ground purely by his own efforts. That would lay the haunting fear Dad spoke of — that you're more solidly, substantially capable. But I'm afraid you can't arrange for his success."

"What do you call being all-time, all-Garrison head boy," demanded Jeff, "if not success?"

"Maybe only a winning smile and smooth talk," Dad said unexpectedly. "Guessing at Paul's point of view, he couldn't be sure that isn't all it amounts to. Guessing again, it may seem temporary. As soon as he graduates, Paul Spencer is just another poor boy looking for a place to begin at the bottom. Facing a comedown is unpleasant, more so if you've been at the top but suspect you never will be again."

Finally Jeff began to nod slowly. "I could almost feel for the guy if he'd act halfway decent. Look, I didn't mean to spoil you folks' evening, but the going was getting tough and it's done me a lot of good."

"Then the evening wasn't spoiled," smiled Mom, and took up her mending.

Dad grinned, "Drop around any time," and returned to his newspaper.

After considering several possibilities Jeff went to the phone, called Bill Hayes, and managed to persuade him that the very thing he wanted to do was serve as chairman of the Cleanup-Paintup parade. They discussed, then, possible members for a committee, announcements for the school bulletin, and working with businessmen through the Chamber of Commerce. Any aspect of the Blossom Festival covered a wide range.

Next day after school was regular meeting time for the quartet. Jeff wondered if Paul would show up. Paul did. His manner was, if anything, more cold, more clipped than before.

So it was going to be like that, far short of Mr. Phillips' dream out of a Wagner opera. Jeff was glad to put music out of his mind for the week end.

At Saturday breakfast Dad said, " We'll go round to the Garrison Garage first thing and get the engine."

" Engine? " For days Jeff had been submerged in affairs of music.

" The one that runs the air compressor at the Mule Ear," Dad explained. " The other day the oil plug in the crankcase worked loose. Vibration, I suppose. Anyway, when Earl Finnegan brought out a load of muck, he found the engine practically afire, running without oil."

" Corn's sake! Must have had practically a complete overhaul job."

" It proved to be cheaper to get another one," said his father. " Fortunately the garage happened to have the motor of an old car. They've honed out the cylinders and put in new pistons and rings. It'll do very well."

When Jeff and his father arrived at the Mule Ear, they found Vince Finnegan spiking down some new rail in the track to the edge of the dump and Earl polishing and oiling the air compressor.

" Tony's in shoring up some more under the old Number Nine Stope," Earl reported. " The air's all right that far."

" Hey, you've been shut down on account of this motor! " Jeff exclaimed in sudden realization.

Dad nodded. " Three and a half days. Without air to blow out the smoke and dust we couldn't even get in for about twenty-four hours after the last round of shots. Then without air we couldn't drill."

All of them fell to work hoisting the new engine into position. As Jeff drove back down Hoodoo Gulch in the gathering dusk that evening, he said, " This has been another setback, hasn't it, Dad? "

" Close to five hundred dollars' worth," Dad admitted. " Costs are running high, and we're still a long way from where the Mule Ear vein ought to be. It has me worried. I'd been hoping not to sink our last dollar in exploration. Have a little in reserve in case we don't find the Mule Ear."

For the first time Dad had put it in words. A stab of dismay went through Jeff so sharply that he turned his thoughts away and changed the subject.

Yet in the weeks that followed the specter of uncertainty hovered around the edges of his mind. Fortunately, they were perhaps the busiest weeks he had ever known. Committee meetings one after another, for he undertook to meet with every festival committee and keep each informed of what the others were doing. Interviews, with Chamber of Commerce members, with school officials, with student organizations. Speeches to the band, to the student body at assembly, and once more before a Chamber of Commerce meeting.

Always in the background, it seemed, lurked the figure of Paul. A grinning — or nodding, winking, and grinning — challenge that loomed even in his dreams and kept him spurred to top effort. Just waiting, Jeff was sure, for him to flop on his face. But not, Jeff had to admit, doing anything to hinder the project.

Why? There was no telling. Maybe Jeff's parting threat

the day of their last big quarrel. More likely, as he understood Paul in the light of Dad and Mom's explanation, something else . . . the desire that came first with Paul to have this year be a rousing record-breaking, never-to-be-forgotten success for Garrison High. As long as Jeff was doing that . . .

Plans for the parade. Plans for the banquet. Plans for the Blossom Ball. Always the rush and drive of rehearsals — soloists practicing, the quartet practicing, the whole band practicing its concert numbers and its marching numbers. The air around school was fairly electric, and Jeff, on the crest of the swell, felt sometimes that he would surely burst between excitement and responsibility.

Then, suddenly, it was the day of the Cleanup-Paintup parade and Jeff, for the first Saturday in he couldn't tell when, had nothing to do but shine his horn, get into his uniform, and show up with the rest of the band. Between now and a week from now there'd be a perfect fever of activity, final preparations. But today all branches of business were laid aside. Even the stores all over town would close from two to four, the streets were hung with bunting overhead, and it was a holiday.

This would be the first full-dress parade in Jeff's band experience. He walked up to the school well ahead of the one thirty deadline. The street for blocks beyond was roped off from traffic and swarming with people in costume getting in position. Big chunks of color were floats draped with crepe paper. Bill Hayes and his group had engineered a big job.

" Hey, boss! "

Rosie Mahoney was checking the roll book as the members arrived. Jeff knew she meant him, as general chairman. You had to get used to Rosie, her dainty small prettiness, her surprising, tremendous voice, and her odd, clipped speech. But she was, underneath, a sincere and earnest person. She'd worked hard and well in preparation for the big dance a week from tonight.

"Letter in this morning's mail," she told Jeff, nerves in her voice. "Oliver's Octet is playing someplace else. Can't come. No band for the Blossom Ball."

"Corn's sake!" exclaimed Jeff. "Not a tie-up at this stage of the game!"

"No less. They've been traveling, and my letter just caught up. I shoulda been on the ball sooner, but I kept hoping — I feel terrible."

"Corn's sake!" Jeff repeated. "Look, couldn't we send to Denver?"

"And pay a hundred and fifty bucks?" she retorted.

Jeff asked, "Then what does the committee want to do?"

"I phoned 'em," said Rosie. "One wants to use the record player, one wants to ask the Legion Airs, and two say ask Spencer's Swingsters."

For a minute Jeff couldn't speak. Rosie's last three words took him like a mule's kick. *Ask Spencer's Swingsters!* Wouldn't that be cozy! When the very reason for their beginning was so that Paul could slap Jeff in the face! If they were the last band on earth . . . Of course Rosie wouldn't know . . .

Holding himself carefully, Jeff asked, "Who are these Legion Airs you mentioned?"

"Six men from the Legion band. They play mostly for older crowds. Not much late stuff. Their stand-by is 'Star Dust.'"

An idea came to Jeff. "What do you want to do, Rosie?" After all, the decision was hers and her committee's.

Rosie shook her brown curls. " No dice, pal. The committee disagrees. The only thing I could get out of 'em was that we'd do whatever you say."

" Oh, no! "

" I know the spot we're putting you in. Paul's treated you stinky ever since you got in town. So O.K., if you say so, I'm ready to use the record player. Only make up your mind as quick as you can, will you? Before my committee splits up over it."

" I'll give you a ring this evening," Jeff promised.

The parade was ready to start, which made a chance for him to think it over a little while. Only why did he have to be the one . . .

Fanfare lifted forward from the trumpet section. The drums set up the rhythm, the whistles blew, batons came down, and they stepped forward. The streets were lined with Saturday crowd, and more. People had come for miles to see this gay event. In spite of the reeling sensation at the back of his head, Jeff couldn't help getting caught up in the swing and spirit of the parade.

People clapped and cheered as they went along, Rosie and Peggy twirling their batons in glittering discs or doing flashy cartwheels out in front. The sidewalks were one continuous bank of noisy approval. There were Mom and Ginny, the latter jumping up and down with excitement, and Mrs. Hardesty and Betty Jean. All the way down Juniper to the stadium it was a triumphal procession.

They turned on River Street across to Main and started back up toward the courthouse at Twelfth. Breath for playing and breath for walking uphill was hard to come by. Horns got heavier, and feet began to feel heat and soreness from pounding the pavement. It was a real relief to wheel into position on the courthouse lawn.

Here a reviewing stand was set up, filled with important people. An announcer manned a microphone and named the floats and the marching groups. From where he stood, Jeff could see the rest of the parade come by, for which he was glad. He'd intended before the march to go along the line and view the turnout, but talking with Rosie . . .

Paul didn't have any such break coming to him. He'd refused to do any of the hard, tedious work of getting ready for the Blossom Festival. He had no right to step in and get the money job, the spotlight job. That was all Paul ever wanted to do anyway — occupy the spotlight. Nuts!

The school debating society went past, and Jeff forgot his problem. The debaters had mounted a pickup truck with what looked like an organ grinder, though a record player furnished the music. At each side of the truck ran debaters in monkey suits, bearing cups and little signs reading: " We are in need — of rooms for visiting band members next Saturday night." A cute stunt Mel had planned! The crowd laughed and teased the monkeys, and some threw pennies.

A record player, though, was always and unmistakably a record player. What it reminded you of was gym class and dancing instruction. For a full-blown, glamour-packed ball, with a queen to crown and out-of-town guests — ugh! The record player was out.

The businessmen had certainly got behind this parade. You wouldn't have thought a town of forty-five hundred could have so many trucks. Nor that crepe paper and bunting would give a truck such tone. The Hardesty Hardware truck was followed by the one from the Mule Ear, borrowed for the occasion. A tremendously long canopy was stretched above both trucks, the cloth one vast splash of color showing all the shades of paint Hardesty's carried. Along the lower edge was lettered: " Clean Up and Paint Up Garrison. Let's

Look Our Best for the Blossom Festival." Maybe Carol's idea!

The Legion band concluded the parade. They were playing as they approached, the "Washington Post" in solid, steady rhythm. Carefully, unexcited. And what was the matter with "Star Dust"? It was a classic of its kind. Only there was no dash, no glamour — Jeff shook his head irritably.

Why couldn't he get his mind off it? Appreciate the enthusiasm of the crowd, the mayor's sonorous proclamation of this as Cleanup-Paintup Blossom Festival Week? The cheering. The splendid job Bill Hayes and his committee had engineered.

Jeff went home and up to his room and propped his feet on his desk. He stared at the wall. Maybe he ought to be noble about this; turn the other cheek and stuff. Only Jeff laid no claims to nobility. Paul Spencer had handed him enough crumby deals. He'd prefer bashing the guy's teeth in to offering him a juicy job where he could hog the spotlight. The thing wasn't worth a second thought . . .

Except that Spencer's Swingsters could do a better job for the Blossom Ball than anybody else.

That was the heck of it. Paul and his bunch could put the Ball over. Jeff had seen Paul lead, seen his way with a crowd. Mr. Hardesty had said Paul had the personality for a band leader. From what Jeff had heard of these little two-bit dances the Swingsters had been playing, probably mostly for experience . . .

Oh, for corn's sake! Jeff got up and clumped down the stairs to the telephone.

"Rosie? This is Jeff. O.K., the boss. Can you think of anybody that'd do as good a job on the Blossom Ball as Spencer's Swingsters?"

"I guess not, darn it," came Rosie's reply.

175

"Then all right, let's get 'em. How much will they cost?"

"Give 'em fifty dollars and they'll think it's Christmas," Rosie predicted. "When you going to ask 'em?"

"I wish," said Jeff, "you'd do that. I'd rather not."

"I'll call the Head Cheese right now," promised Rosie.

Jeff went in to dinner. At least he didn't have to worry about the Blossom Ball any more. Being Paul's show, Paul would put it over. And how! There'd be plenty of other things for Jeff to look after during the coming week.

CHAPTER 12

As Jeff went into band Monday, Rosie said, "Everything's under control, boss."

"Meaning," Jeff interpreted, "you got the Swingsters engaged to play the Ball O.K.?"

She nodded. "I told 'em it was you who decided—"

"If there's anybody else you'd rather get," a voice said, "you're free to change your mind."

Jeff spun around to meet the cold eyes of Paul Spencer, who had just entered the room. The back of Jeff's neck grew hot.

"You think I'd ask you as good politics?" he snapped back.

Rosie whispered urgently, "Break it up, you guys!"

The room had gone quiet, though the bell had not rung nor the whistle blown. All eyes were on Jeff and Paul, both of whom drew attention these days, Jeff realized, for more reasons than their conspicuous height. The old taut conflict could once more be felt, strumming tight.

A sort of dreary anger seized Jeff as they moved away to take their places. He was fed up, and Mom's word that Paul couldn't help being like that was remote comfort. He promised himself that once this Blossom Festival was over, he was going to shut Paul Spencer's trap for him, whether it knocked any sense into his head or not. Let somebody else be understanding for a while!

The band's rehearsal was the poorest in weeks. Jeff was still sore about it when he got home. As he arrived, Dad drove up in the Mule Ear truck.

"If you have an hour free from festivalizing," Mr. Miles grinned at his son, "how's about getting the truck serviced and then going on to Hardesty's for a load of mine supplies I've ordered? I have some bookkeeping to do, and I'd like to get an early start in the morning."

"Good deal," said Jeff, and swung into the cab. He drove around to the filling station, pulled up beside the gas pump, and got out as the white-coveralled attendant came around the rear.

"Fill 'er up?"

Jeff could only stand in stunned silence. It took him seconds to hoist his jaw back into place and say weakly, "Yeah, fill 'er up." The attendant was Brick Lassiter!

Brick looked up from the gas hose with defiance. "Never thought I'd come to this, hunh?"

Jeff felt his face redden. "You have a bet on, or something?"

"Heck, no. I'm working for the dough."

Jeff didn't get it at all. "You're away ahead of me. Mind spelling it out slow, or is it none of my business?"

Brick started to check the tires, moving rapidly but with a slight limp. Seeing the limp, Jeff said, "I'll do that."

"Squirrel food. Whose job is this?" returned Brick. "And it's no secret. I drew a fine, and damages to pay, out of that accident. Gonna handle it myself. Keeps Pop from lecturing on life. You need a quart of oil."

"O.K.," said Jeff. He couldn't think of any further comment. Brick's gruff manner didn't invite it, anyway.

178

The red head emerged from under the hood. "That battery's gonna have to be replaced before cold weather sets in again. I'd like to make the deal. I get a percentage on extra stuff like that."

Jeff overcame his amazement to say, "I'll use my influence." Then, cautiously, he asked, "Meaning you intend to stay with this?"

"Why not? I like work around cars, and here I don't have to take any favors from anybody." He completed Jeff's sales ticket.

Jeff signed. "Strictly business, hunh?"

"That's it. I go for it. Take after Pop, I guess. Say, it was a nice piece of business you threw our way Saturday night." At Jeff's blank look Brick explained, "I'm business manager for Spencer's Swingsters."

Numb to surprise by this time, Jeff could only say, "I'm getting out of here before you start to sell me a hot rod or something."

"I could get you a good deal on one." And Brick's old booming laugh followed Jeff out to the truck.

Corn's sake, if this wasn't a way for the Brick thing to turn out! Why, you could — no, the guy had always been likable. You could respect him now. That was the difference. And he was enjoying himself, you could tell, in a way that wasn't hopped up as it had somehow seemed in the days of the unlimited allowance and maroon convertible. This was real, and Brick had done it himself. Suppose something of the kind was what Dad and Mom were talking about in connection with Paul? But of course Paul wasn't changing a bit.

This week, though, was for action, not heavy thinking. On Tuesday the students voted on Garrison's candidate for Queen of the Blossom Ball. It was Carol Hardesty! That

179

pleased Jeff immensely, what time he had to consider it. Wednesday there were final meetings of some committees, and the next day of the others.

Jeff was almost late for dinner Thursday. Still not enough rooms promised. As soon as he could eat —

As Jeff came through the door Ginny charged him, grabbed his neck and swung in a circle, a ceremony she had stopped performing in recent years. It almost knocked him flat.

Then there was Dad with a foot-wide grin and eyes crinkling; Mom flushed and gay and pretty, almost giggling; Perry circling in their midst, barking as if he'd cornered the chipmunk market.

"What," Jeff demanded as he regained his balance, "has broken loose, for corn's sake?"

"The Mule Ear! The Mule Ear!" chanted Ginny.

"The Mule Ear what?"

"We think we've found the rest of it." Dad's drawl was as triumphant as Perry's bark.

"You mean — Cheese!"

"It means we stay in Garrison!" Mom declared, her voice unsteady with happiness. "Always. Right in this house."

"And Tony and Elfida are getting married," Ginny chanted. "We're all going to be filthy rich," she chanted further. "And —"

"Now hold on," said Dad. "Nobody's going to be rich, either plain or filthy. We didn't open a cavern of gold nuggets. We might even be wrong that it's the Mule Ear vein."

"But you don't think so," Jeff charged. "Tell me about it."

"We hit a few stringers day before yesterday," Dad said, "but it was too soon. I didn't dare mention it and raise false hopes. We did start drilling and shooting as fast as we could, not bothering to muck out completely. Today we got into the vein. Runs up to thirteen inches thick. I'm pretty sure it's the Mule Ear, in spite of its location."

" What about the location? "

" Fifty-eight feet closer than I'd calculated," answered Dad. " But I sampled it, and sent Tony over to Murdock for an assay. He got back just awhile ago. This ore will pay the cost of mining, and transportation to the smelter at Womack, and refining, and still leave us with a respectable profit. A business with a steady income as long as we're taking out ore like this."

" Not meaning to sound silly," Jeff said, " what does happen when the mine is worked out? They all are, in time, aren't they? "

Mom interposed: " Jeff, hang up your jacket and come on to dinner. We're having steak and mushrooms to celebrate."

" All mines are worked out eventually," Dad resumed when they were seated. " In the meantime, other things happen. First, there will be a big increase in mining activity around here as soon as news of the Mule Ear gets out. Modern version of the old gold rush."

" That'll be something to see."

" Before long it will be possible to hire plenty of miners and then I think I'll turn over the Mule Ear to Tony and a crew to operate. There'll be an urgent demand for mine valuation and surveying, which of course is exactly my line of work."

" What about the Finnegans? " Ginny asked.

" They're very anxious now to get back to Finnegan's Wake," smiled Dad. " They'll be leaving soon. Another thing I might do is buy the old Garrison Assay Office and reopen it. Then I can always be on the lookout for another property to develop like the Mule Ear."

"Corn's sake, doesn't everything look good! Mom, is it O.K. if I skip dessert? Emergency. We're still short of rooms for forty visiting bandsmen. Mel and I got some Chamber of Commerce men to help, and a bunch of students. We're going out in teams this evening for a house-to-house canvass. We'll meet at Mel's place afterward to total up, and I expect there'll be refreshments."

"Then I won't worry about your nourishment," laughed Mom. "But I will be glad when you don't have to keep going so hard."

"After this Mule Ear news," Jeff grinned, "I could keep going indefinitely."

To keep going indefinitely seemed almost what was required of him. How there could be so many last-minute things to do . . .

After a space of time it was Saturday, half past twelve. Four hundred and forty-two high school folks, nine directors, six judges, and a committee of five from the Chamber of Commerce were filing into the Garrison High cafeteria for the welcome luncheon. Jeff took the figures from the registration desk in Senior Circle upstairs to Dick, who was perspiringly wondering how the teachers daily got five hundred people in and out of this place at each of two lunch periods.

"Holy cow!" gasped Dick. "How many does that add up to? A lot more than four hundred and fifty, anyway. The head cook'll be wild. Go see if you can tear down to the bakery or delicatessen or something for her, will you, Jeff? Or it's my neck."

The cook, however, apparently was somewhat experienced at this sort of thing. All she'd be short was two pies, for which Jeff did tear down to the bakery, appreciating Dad's thoughtfulness in leaving him the car.

Jeff's afternoon went to helping the housing committee. At least one Garrison student went with every visitor or group of visitors to the home where they were to stay, made the introductions, and saw them settled. That wouldn't have been required, but it gave a nice tone to things. No time or effort was too much if the Blossom Festival was made more nearly perfect.

Music came from the study halls as Jeff went in and out of the school building. Soloists playing before pairs of judges for ratings . . . arrangements by Henrietta's committee. Jeff took a fellow from Colorow High and one from the little town of Riseup to his own house for the night.

By six the last out-of-towner had been placed, and Jeff had time to wash up at home on his way back to school for the banquet. The cafeteria tables had been transformed with white cloths and candles and sprays of orchard bloom. The Pep Club girls were colorful waitresses in their purple skirts and gold sweaters. And as the crowd gathered, the room became brilliant. There must have been at least a dozen different colors in the nine combinations.

Food was good too. What would they have done without Chamber of Commerce backing? Then Jeff caught a sign from Rosie and slipped out to help the committee put the finishing touches on the gym for the Blossom Ball. The banqueters would be another hour, at least. Each school had five minutes to put on a skit introducing its candidate for Queen of the Blossom Ball. Jeff would have liked to see how Garrison presented Carol.

The gym — well, it was no longer a great barren cavern. It was a fairyland of spring, festooned with cherry blossoms and apple blossoms. A stepladder rose towering out of sight among the flowers. Presently Mr. Collins descended the ladder, carrying an extension cord.

"Soon as I get this one set," the old gentleman offered, "I can fix the band platform, and that does it."

"You've certainly gone to a lot of trouble," said Rosie.

"I hope it wasn't too much," Jeff added, a bit anxiously.

"Naw, I'm sound as a nut since I swore off hot dogs and Cokes," chuckled Mr. Collins. "Never did think a dance looked right with high-powered bulbs glarin' away up there, and I sort of owe the band a little favor."

By the time they'd put the last touches on the queen's throne and arranged the chaperons' chairs, all of them had to hustle home to change and get back to take invitations at the door.

Must be nearly a thousand people at the Ball, Jeff estimated. Mostly they went by him in a blur as he handed out ballots on which they voted for the queen. Some he saw as individuals.

"Who shall I — I mean, for whom shall I vote?" someone laughed. It was Carol, lovely in a formal dress with flowing skirt and close-fitting bodice — Jeff thought that was the name for it. She was with her parents, but she wore an orchid which blended with the color of her dress and which, Jeff guessed, she'd received from Paul.

"Let me mark your ballot?" he suggested, but she laughed again and shook her head.

"The girl from Sniktau, their drum majorette, is pretty and talented," Carol declared.

Neither as pretty nor as talented, Jeff was about to say — but the Hardestys had moved on with the crowd.

When Jeff got inside the gym, almost the first person he saw was Brick Lassiter. Jeff frowned. Brick wouldn't have received a bid. Then Jeff remembered. Brick was business manager for Spencer's Swingsters and had come, no doubt, with the band. He wasn't dancing, but talking vigorously with a large-waisted man who must be the parent of some visitor. Maybe selling the man a new battery?

Soon Jeff forgot Brick in watching and listening to Spencer's Swingsters. What a combo! There were a sax, another guy who doubled on clarinet and sax, a piano thumper, and a vibraphone player. Two trumpets, who were only soso in the school band, on this type of music gave out with zing. The trombonist whom Mr. Phillips assigned to second chair was making like Dorsey now. Walt Terry, surrounded by enough traps to outfit an impi of Zulus, was really jumping. Underlying the whole effect, you could feel the solid leadership of Paul's sousaphone, its imposing bell glowing in the spotlight.

They played the late, bright music. Played it sweet and swinging, and the youthful crowd loved it, loved Paul and the way he acted out a tune all over as he led. The infectious nod, wink, and grin! The palsy, folksy little commentaries between numbers!

Periodically he'd ask, " All you nice people having fun? " They'd roar, " YES," and clap and whistle. Old swoon-maker Spencer lapped up the adulation. Corn's sake, this was his dish! The bell of his horn glowed no brighter than he did when the spotlight was on him.

Suddenly the two trumpeters rose and sent forth a blast of fanfare. Paul held up both hands for silence.

" All you nice people remember you voted for a queen as you came in? The tally is complete, certified by the judges. So here she is, ladies and gentlemen, the Queen of the Blossom Ball by your choice — and I might tell you confidentially, by my choice — Miss . . . *Carol* . . . HARDESTY! "

The trumpets burst forth again but were drowned out in a roar from the crowd. Paul stepped down from the stand and gave his arm to Carol, who was smiling, dazzlingly radiant. Jeff added his bit to the applause. The Swingsters hit into triumphal music without Paul's leadership while he escorted Carol to the queen's throne.

The high school principal presented the crown to Carol and corsages to the other eight candidates. Photographers' flash bulbs flared. The Swingsters struck up again and the grand march began, Paul and Carol leading, followed by the other royal misses and their escorts. Jeff saw Rosie standing at one side and, crossing to her, crooked his arm in offer.

" Sure," the girl accepted. " Us working people ought to at least get in the mob scene." They joined the promenade.

After the grand march some of the people serving refreshments came to ask Rosie about something. Jeff moved among the crowd. He glimpsed Carol dancing her honor turn with the principal, and again when Paul descended from the stand once more to claim a dance with her.

Jeff had never seen so many people all so gay, having, without exception, so good a time. Certainly the Blossom Ball would never have been such a glory hour if the Legion Airs, or even Oliver's Octet, had been engaged to play. It was Paul who made the occasion. This night was his.

After breakfast next morning Jeff drove out with the two fellows who were his guests to see the sights. The high drive over Ruby Ridge, the tunnels and towering dumps of the old Del Oro Mine, the lumber mills, and the abandoned coke ovens that had once been a part of Garrison's industry. Talking, he told himself, like a pamphlet for tourists. Well, why not? He was a permanent resident of the place.

" Your school certainly must have a live student government," suggested the fellow from Colorow. " Your head boy's really got it."

" It must be great," said the one from Riseup, " to have a

leader who doesn't wait for the faculty to begin everything. No wonder you people can stage terrific things like this Blossom Festival."

So now the Blossom Festival was Paul's!

No percentage, though, Jeff reminded himself, in being bitter. After a moment's reflection he said, " Spencer's doing a nice job with the swing band too."

How good a job, Jeff wondered, would Paul do with the quartet where the spotlight simply couldn't be all his? It would be known soon. Ensembles started playing for ratings at nine thirty this morning. The Garrison quartet was scheduled to go on at ten. He took his guests back to the house, brushed up his uniform, and set forth carrying his horn.

He and Henrietta and Carol, the latter still starry-eyed from last night's triumph, were gathered in the hall outside Study 223, and Jeff's watch said nine fifty-nine before Paul appeared.

" Hi! " he exclaimed breathlessly. " Hi! Hi! Boy! Boy-oh-boy! "

Jeff stared. The guy seemed ready to pop.

" What in the world? " asked Carol.

" The Swingsters! Boy-oh-boy! You know Whitehall Lodge? "

Henrietta said, " You mean the big resort hotel near Murdock? "

" That's it. Listen, the Swingsters have got an offer to play the Starlight Terrace job there every night for three weeks this summer! "

" Why, Paul, how — "

" Get it? Eighty bucks a night for twenty-one nights! Brick saw Mr. Whitehall at the dance last night, and after he heard us — They'll have the contract ready to sign this afternoon!"

Jeff recalled the portly gentleman whose ear Brick had been bending. "A good thing Brick was on the job," he observed, thinking of the redhead's newly found business acumen.

Abruptly quiet settled upon Paul. "The big thing," he said in a low voice, "we were playing the job. In your place, Miles . . ."

The sentence trailed off, but there was no mistaking what Paul meant. *In your place, Miles, I wouldn't have chosen Spencer's Swingsters. That was big of you.*

Jeff suspected his ears. It was the first time Paul had ever acknowledged that anything Jeff did was worth noticing. Was three weeks' work so important —

"I'm just catching up," said Carol. "This could lead to big things later on."

"See what I mean?" Paul exulted. "Not clerking in the men's department at the Garrison Dry Goods. Maybe leading the band at the Broadmoor! Who knows?"

So it wasn't merely those twenty-one days. Paul seemed to see ahead along solid ground toward his future, to have laid a haunting fear of coming down to begin at the bottom after graduation —

Why, Jeff realized, he was thinking in the words of Dad and Mom! Had this thing given Paul that deep-down confidence in himself which the folks thought he had to have before he could overcome a secret dread? Last night had been a terrific triumph for Paul, more than Jeff would have dreamed even though he was the one who'd chosen the Swingsters. He ought to say something to Paul, but —

"Brass quartet from Garrison." The words from the study-hall door as it opened jolted them all.

As they moved automatically toward the door, Paul

stepped forward and faced the other three. "Look, guys, I don't know how to say this." He spoke in a hurried undertone. "If it hadn't been for me, this quartet could have meant more. For what it's worth, I want you to know Spencer's with you, all of you, all the way."

Then it *had* happened. Thanks be, Jeff thought, he had talked it out with the folks, so that he had some foggy notion of what was going on. Otherwise he'd think it was only a sort of I-love-everybody celebration of a sixteen-hundred-dollar contract.

They were in the front of the room, facing Mr. Phillips and three other directors and two judges and a scattering of students. Jeff remembered, *I could almost feel for the guy if he'd act halfway decent.*

Then Carol touched, softly, the first dotted eighth note and the sixteenth, and as the others joined their parts to hers, in the space of an instant they were not four, but one. Together! One swift, precise, clear fire of golden harmony that lifted and soared in beauty, living out the moving tones in an experience of music's universal language.

At its end they seemed to come down floating out of exaltation to find the handful of students cheering wildly and the judges nodding and smiling and Mr. Phillips beaming upon them with a grin that was neither dry nor humorous.

A judge said: "Rating of One. Excellent!"

They looked at each other with dazed eyes, awed.

The Garrison stadium that afternoon was packed, both sides, plank on plank. Jeff was gratified at this attendance, not only because the Chamber of Commerce certainly was taking in enough admissions to defray much of their expense but also because all these people placed so much importance on the event.

In the middle of the playing field was a vast expanse of

189

board platform, and scattered around the green were vivid masses of color where the nine bands were gathering. Each band would march and play a concert number, and finally all nine would be combined in mass concert under each director in turn.

Mr. Phillips held up his hand. "We go first," he called. "Host school in the tough spot. It's turning out to be a grand festival. Now let's not let the folks down."

Suddenly Paul was beside the conductor. "It *is* a grand festival, maestro." He flashed his nod, wink, and grin. "But it strikes me nobody's said anything about the guy who's responsible for putting it over. Step out here, Jeff, and hear what this gang has to give you in the way of a hand."

The unexpectedness of it struck silence over the band and left Jeff paralyzed. Then, as somebody urged him forward, they broke out in a storm of clapping, and when Paul lifted Jeff's right arm in a signal of triumph, when all at once they understood that the old friction was gone, the applause rose to a whistling frenzy. Jeff could only stand and grin, saying: "Thanks. Thanks." He could not be heard.

Before he could recover, they were on their way. Moving down the field to the *slash ka-boom slash slash boom boom!* of the drums with snap, dash, confidence. Knowing they were good. Feeling their hard-won mastery and their unity now. The strains of "National Emblem" rode the air triumphantly.

They took seats at the front of the great stage and went into "Poet and Peasant." Jeff filled the bore of his big horn full and let it sing from his heart. He reached out and touched with sound the sounds of Carol and Henrietta and Paul, so that together they fronted and carried all the rest magnificently along. Mr. Phillips' rugged features shone as he swung the stick.

The massed concert, later, was unlike anything Jeff had ever known. He sat at the head of a triple row of baritones, seventeen in all. At the first downsweep of the baton, with Eagle City's director on the stand, the mighty surge of sound seemed to pick them all up bodily and hold them suspended on its rolling crest.

The Blossom Festival was over. What a day! What a festival! What a *year!*

The visiting players trooped toward the buses that would take them back to their home towns. The Garrison kids naturally gravitated together, surrounding Mr. Phillips.

" O.K.! O.K.! " he grinned at them. " Your rating is One, and it should be. Thanks. Thanks to the whole doggoned, ornery lot of you! And if anybody's absent tomorrow, I'll clobber him. We've got a commencement program to rehearse."

Cheers and groans and good-natured " Yaak, yaak! " followed him as he went toward his family and his sandy hair was lost to view.

" Let's go up to the Knot Inn and celebrate."

" Sure. Henrietta can have *two* ice-cream cones! "

" Come on, Paul. Lead out."

" Sorry, gang." The nod, wink, and grin were different, somehow. It came to Jeff: the gesture was happy now. Not just an anxious effort to please. Paul said: " I've got to see a man about a contract. Got a lo-ong way to go." And he hurried off.

It came about — well, maybe Jeff did walk a little extra fast — that he was going along beside Carol. " I never heard of a queen," he stated, " who carried her own trumpet."

" That's nothing," she laughed up at him. " I never heard of a queen who took queening seriously that even played a trumpet." But she gave him the instrument, which he carried in his left hand while his baritone was in his right, and she fell into step beside him.

"Don't lose your balance, there, Jeff," somebody advised. Referring, maybe, to the difference in size of the two instruments.

"I hope you're not allergic to corn," declared the girl. "I think it's nice of you to carry it."

"Shucks," grinned Jeff, "I agreed to be a good neighbor."

"So you did. Way back about Christmas."

"Right after Thanksgiving," he remembered.

"Anyway, the thing about neighbors," Carol smiled, "they're sure to get better acquainted as they go along."

Jeff's number twelves didn't touch the sidewalk for blocks, not that he knew of.

"Hey, Jeff." That was Mel. "What you doing, say about Wednesday night?"

"Nothing, I guess."

"Know what? I've been thinking we ought to get together, all the kids that worked on festival committees. Just for a good time, after the toil we've been through. I've got clearance on using our rumpus room."

"That's a wonderful idea," cried Carol. "And we girls could bring food."

"Then pass the word, will you, Jeff? You know all the guys."

He knew all the guys! Mel wouldn't realize what that meant.

"Why, sure," Jeff grinned. "I'll ask the committee members. And if you want to ask anybody yourself, I expect there'd be no objections." You could kid like that, among friends!